SASSY LADY

Becky Barker

A KISMET™ Romance

METEOR PUBLISHING CORPORATION
Bensalem, Pennsylvania

KISMET™ is a trademark of Meteor Publishing Corporation

First Printing February 1992.

ISBN: 1-878702-79-3

Printed in the United States of America

Rachel, ewe lamb, I love you.
Happy Birthday Sweet Sixteen.

BECKY BARKER

Becky Barker lives in rural Ohio with her husband,
Buzz, and their three children: Rachel, Amanda, and
Thad. Becky is a staff writer for a weekly newspaper
and is an advisor for the Central Ohio chapter of the
Romance Writers of America. She has been an avid
reader of romance since grade school and considers
herself one of those lucky people whose life has been
filled with music, laughter, and love.

Other books by Becky Barker:

ONE

"Hey, Curt!"

Maggie Malone flinched when the proprietor of Larson's general store bellowed across the room on her behalf.

"Curt! This little lady is tryin' to find the McCain ranch. You headin' back out there now?"

"Please, I don't want to trouble anyone. I'll be fine if you can just point me in the right direction," Maggie insisted.

"No trouble," the proprietor spoke for the other man. "Curt's a foreman at the ranch."

The man named Curt came into view as he made his way to the checkout counter where Maggie was standing. She looked into his eyes and her breathing faltered. The foreman struck her as one of those men who didn't even like to give you the time of day, let alone have a stranger thrust on him.

"I'm not going to the ranch, but I'm heading north," he told the proprietor while his light blue eyes took in Maggie's petite stature and mass of auburn hair.

7

Maggie assumed the McCain ranch was north because the proprietor she'd asked for directions nodded
his head in satisfaction.

"Thanks," she returned politely, not wanting assistance from a man who obviously didn't want to give it.
"But there's no need to escort me to the McCains'. I
don't have any trouble following instructions."

"The ranch ain't hard to find," the helpful proprietor
explained, "but there's a storm brewin' and a wind
blowin' from the north. It ain't good to be roamin' the
countryside alone."

Maggie swallowed more words of protest. She'd
lived most of her life in Chicago, so the wind factor
didn't worry her. What worried her was the cool perusal
she was getting from the big cowboy who stood a foot
taller than her five feet and looked at her as though she
were a troublesome insect.

His unfriendly attitude was foreign to her and left
her momentarily at a loss for words: an occurrence she
couldn't remember experiencing in all of her twenty-
six years.

"I'll follow you out of town and direct you to the
ranch," the foreman said in a deep baritone, his eyes
very cool. His face was deeply tanned, with fine lines
about the eyes from squinting in the sun. The rest of
his features could have been cast in stone.

"I'd appreciate that," Maggie responded. The cowboy had already turned and was heading for the door.
She assumed she should follow. "Thank you," she
threw over her shoulder to the proprietor as she tried
to catch up with her rude guide.

Curt stopped at the door and waited for her. He
pushed his hat onto his head and shifted the grocery

bag to his left arm so that he could hold the door for the little lady.

They were both caught by wind the instant they left the store. The building afforded them some protection, yet Maggie's skirt whirled wildly around her legs. She quickly buttoned her trench coat from neck to hem. Most of her hair was tucked into her coat, but she still had to grab a handful to keep it from obscuring her vision.

"Is that your car?" the cowboy asked, inclining his head toward her small red sports car.

Maggie nodded and was sure he grunted his disapproval.

"You must be a friend of Tara's," the cowboy surmised, raising his voice to be heard over the rising sound of the wind.

Maggie dared to look him directly in the eyes. "Tara?"

"Mrs. McCain," he explained succinctly.

Shaking her head, Maggie corrected him. "I've never met Mrs. McCain. I've spoken to her on the phone, but I'm going to the ranch for a job interview, not as a guest."

Maggie hadn't thought it possible, but the cowboy's expression seemed to grow more grim. Maybe he'd hoped she was here for a very short visit. She wondered how he could have taken such an immediate dislike to her. She rarely affected people in that fashion. She was a regular Miss Congeniality.

Curt shifted the grocery bag again and gently took hold of Maggie's right arm, preparing to walk her to her car.

"That blue pickup truck is mine," he told her, motioning toward the truck parked several spaces behind her car. "Turn right at the traffic light and left at the next intersection. You'll be on the main road. The McCain ranch is twenty miles out of town. I'll follow you for about fifteen miles."

Maggie wanted to tell him it wasn't necessary, but as soon as they both stepped from the protection of the building, they were blasted by a gust of wind that literally took her breath away and slammed her against the cowboy's rock-hard body. Even though they were both wearing coats, she was stunned by the impact of her soft body against his hard one.

Pushing herself away from him, Maggie quickly regained her balance with the assistance of one of the cowboy's strong arms. Her eyes were apologetic as they met his.

"Sorry," was all she could manage.

Curt walked her to her car and made sure she was safely behind the wheel, then headed for his truck. The wind was getting so strong that his heavy vehicle was gently rocking.

Tossing the groceries to the passenger side, he folded his long body into the driver's seat and frowned at the thought of how the wind would batter the lightweight vehicle.

As soon as the sports car pulled from the curb, Curt put the truck in gear and followed. The little lady made all the proper turns and soon they were headed north, but fierce gusts of wind made the small car weave dangerously.

Maggie gave her full attention to keeping her car on the right side of the road. She was used to driving into a strong wind, but mostly in the city. Out here she was getting hit full force from the front and then getting caught in whirlwinds.

There was nothing but open range on either side of the highway and no protection from the wind's ferocity. Every few miles she passed a tree with a broad trunk and full, swaying branches, but they didn't look too safe, either.

The sky was growing blacker and Maggie could tell she was heading straight into the storm system. A few giant raindrops gradually increased to a heavy shower and then a downpour. Visibility rapidly decreased and Maggie strained to control the car. A glance at the odometer showed that she'd only driven ten miles from Larson, but it seemed much farther.

Hands locked around the steering wheel, Maggie's pulse accelerated along with her anxiety. Her body grew taut with tension and her eyes began to burn from the strain of trying to see beyond the windshield.

She was glad that a road sign warned her of a sharp left turn, but she was unprepared when the powerful north wind caught her broadside. The car rocked violently and she feared that it would actually be knocked off the road.

She slowed the vehicle to a crawl when terrifying flashes of lightning began to split the inky darkness of the sky. The sound of thunder reverberated all around her and was nearly as deafening as the pounding of her own pulse.

Another gust of wind rocked the car and Maggie decided she wasn't going any further until the storm abated. When she caught sight of a huge tree on her side of the road, she slowed the car.

The tree might attract lightning, but the protection it afforded from the wind was preferable to being rolled around the countryside like a tumbleweed. She switched on her emergency flashers and pulled to a stop, sighing with relief as the tree created a partial windbreak.

She'd nearly forgotten the cowboy until his pickup truck pulled alongside her car. He rolled down the window on the passenger side, and Maggie reluctantly opened her window a crack so that she could hear him.

Needle-sharp, freezing rain lashed her face and neck as she strained to hear what the cowboy was saying.

"You can't stay under that tree," he growled. "My place is a couple miles down the road. There's another curve that will head us north into the wind again. If you follow me, my truck will block some of the wind."

He didn't give Maggie a chance to argue, just rolled up the window and pulled in front of her. She grudgingly put her car in gear and followed.

Visibility did improve a little when she could follow his taillights. As soon as they rounded a sharp right curve, her car stopped rocking so violently. His wide vehicle blocked the worst of the wind, but the rain pelted her windshield relentlessly and Maggie allowed herself a groan of distress.

How did she always manage to get into these kinds of predicaments? Her family said it was because she was so impetuous, independent, and headstrong, but she didn't know how to be anything else. Besides, how could she have known that driving to the McCain ranch would be such a nightmare? It was September and she hadn't expected the weather to be a problem.

When the cowboy's brake lights flashed, Maggie realized the truck was turning into a driveway. She drove through a gate and over metal cattle guards. Lightning flashed, enabling her to see the shape of a two-story building about a half mile ahead of the truck.

Another gust of wind rocked the car, and Maggie's

heart leapt into her throat. Her stomach was rolling, and she prayed that the car wouldn't do the same before she made it to shelter.

She felt the crunch of gravel beneath her tires give way to smoother pavement, and then watched as the cowboy's truck pulled into a carport attached to a house. There was enough room to fit her car beside the truck. She parked, shut off her lights and engine, then collapsed against the steering wheel in relief.

"Are you all right?" the cowboy demanded as he threw open her door and bent down to peer inside.

Maggie turned her head, and found herself looking directly into the cowboy's ruggedly handsome face and piercing eyes. A shiver raced over her, but she attributed it to the cold, damp air that rushed around her.

"I'm fine, just relieved to be sitting still," she commented huskily.

"We'd better get in the house," he insisted, taking hold of her arm and leaving her little choice but to cooperate.

Maggie barely had time to grab her keys and pocketbook before she was pulled from the car and practically carried to the door of the house. The cowboy's big body absorbed the brunt of the pelting rain, but she was still drenched before they managed to get through the door and onto a closed porch.

"Is this your house?" she asked as they shook some of the water from their bodies.

"Yes," Curt responded. He wasn't thrilled with having a female guest—his very first—but he had little choice in the matter. Another couple of miles and her car would have overturned or sunk axle deep in the water beginning to rush across the road.

"You can leave your coat out here to dry," he told her as he hung his over a hook on the wall.

Maggie nodded, not trusting herself to speak. Her teeth were beginning to chatter, and she was shivering with cold. Her coat had kept most of her dress dry, but her hair, hemline, legs, and feet were soaked.

Curt took her coat and spread it over the back of the only chair on the porch. Then he opened the door to the kitchen and ushered his guest inside where it was a little warmer, but not much.

"I'll get a fire started in the fireplace," he told her, noticing how chilled she was. "This way."

Maggie followed him through the spacious kitchen into an even more spacious living room. Half of one wall was covered with a stone fireplace, and she followed as he moved toward it.

Wrapping her arms tightly about her, she looked around the room. She had an insatiable curiosity, and it was kicking into high gear, even though her main concern was getting warm.

The cowboy's house was obviously still under construction. The air smelled of new wood and sawdust. The walls and hardwood floors were bare, and the only piece of furniture in the room was a big, leather sofa. She'd seen appliances in the kitchen, but the only furnishings in there were a wooden table with a couple of straight-backed chairs. If he lived here, he must like to rough it.

Maggie wondered if he had a wife and family. She glanced at his left hand as he lit a match and noted that he wasn't wearing a ring. That wasn't a guarantee, but it made her feel both relief and chagrin. While she didn't like the idea of being totally alone with a swinging single, she didn't really like the idea that he might have a wife waiting for him.

As soon as Curt had the fire steadily burning, he turned his attention back to his guest. She had looked small in her coat, but without it, she looked really tiny. Despite the mature, hourglass figure, he couldn't remember ever seeing anyone with features so small and delicate.

Though her stature was slight, the brilliance of her dark eyes assured him that she was self-confident and strong-minded. She'd battled the Oklahoma elements with an iron determination that proved she wasn't as fragile as her appearance suggested.

Curt took the two blankets from the sofa and spread one on the floor in front of the fireplace. Then he stepped close to Maggie and wrapped the second blanket about her shoulders. She shivered, still not speaking, but she gave him a warm smile for his thoughtfulness.

Curt frowned. The smile was innocent and not the least bit flirtatious, but it sent a current of powerful emotion racing through him. She smelled femininely sweet, and he found himself reacting to her as he hadn't reacted to any woman for a long time. He didn't like it.

"You can sit in front of the fireplace as long as you don't get too close. I don't have a screen for it yet."

Maggie nodded, stepped out of her shoes, pulled the blanket tightly around her shoulders, and dropped to the floor in front of the fire. Her shivering gradually abated, and she felt life coming back into her frozen limbs. She hadn't realized how cold she was until she began to thaw.

Drawing the blanket closer, Maggie inhaled a musky

scent that she knew must belong to her host. There had been a couple of times when she'd been close enough to feel the heat of his body and to smell the unique, masculine scent of him. Her sense of smell was acute, and she found unexpected comfort in burying her face in the stranger's blanket.

Maggie couldn't explain, even to herself, why she wasn't alarmed by the strange turn of events; but she was temporarily content to sit in front of the fire and let the sight and scent of her host penetrate her senses. The cowboy wasn't like anyone she'd ever met.

He had a gorgeous physique: long legs, strong thighs, slim waist, and wonderfully wide shoulders. Maggie let her eyes slowly devour him while he had his back turned. She couldn't remember ever meeting a man that was put together as beautifully.

"The proprietor of the store called you Curt. Would you mind my asking your full name?" she inquired, watching him as he carefully added a big log to the kindling.

"Hayden." His response was as curt as his name, and Maggie was a bit annoyed when he didn't offer more information or ask her name. She decided not to introduce herself.

"You mentioned that this is your house. Do you live here?"

Curt rose and walked to a window. "I live on the McCain ranch most of the time, but I'm trying to get this place finished before winter." If today was an example of the winter to come, it would be a long, stormy one.

"You're doing the carpentry work on the house?"

"Yes."

"You're working alone?"

"Yes."

Maggie wasn't one to be put off by a few monosyllabic replies. "You didn't build the whole house by yourself, did you?"

The amazement in her tone drew Curt's attention back to his pretty guest. "Some of the ranch staff helped me get it under roof last summer, but it's taken me all year to get the electricity and plumbing finished and the furnace installed."

"You did all those things?" Maggie asked, her eyes wide with surprise. She knew people still helped build their own homes, but she'd never met anyone who had the skills to do all the construction work.

"It's cheaper that way," Curt said, flipping on a light to dispel the growing darkness. It was late afternoon, but the sky was midnight dark.

Maggie looked toward the beamed ceiling as the overhead light came on. The light had six separate globes attached to a wagon wheel suspended from the ceiling by a heavy chain.

She'd never seen such a fixture, but she liked it. She also liked the open beams of the ceiling, and the second story loft that circled most of the living room. There was an open staircase that curved in a spiral to the second floor.

"You really did all this?" she repeated, impressed and not shy about revealing her amazement.

"Most of it," Curt told her, turning away from the appealing light in her dark brown eyes.

"The furnace is new and I haven't used it much, but I'll turn it on. It will get really cold in here before long."

"It's still summertime," complained Maggie.

"The heat just makes the storms more violent," he

countered, crossing the living room and opening the door to a large closet where the furnace was housed.

Maggie heard the hum of the equipment as Curt turned it on and thought he must be a good carpenter to handle any project that needed to be done. The furnace worked, and the lighting seemed to be installed properly.

On the other hand, the argumentative side of her brain suggested, he could be lying to impress her. This might not even be his house. He hadn't used a key to enter and they might both be trespassing.

The store proprietor had called him by name and had told her he was a foreman for the McCains. Of course, they could be in cahoots, kidnapping unsuspecting young women and selling them into slavery. There was no end to the possibilities. There never was where Maggie's imagination was concerned. The fact remained that she wasn't the least bit frightened or uneasy about her host and his lovely house.

"What time were you expected at the ranch?"

Curt's question broke into Maggie's thoughts, and she didn't take time to consider her response. "They're not expecting me until tomorrow. I'm a day ahead of schedule, but Mrs. McCain said to come to the ranch as soon as I got to Larson."

Maggie mentally cursed her forthright reply as she realized what she'd just admitted to a total stranger. She wished she'd learn how to be more evasive.

Curt's mouth curved slightly. His guest obviously wasn't one of those people who lied about everything and considered the consequences later. She was just the opposite: probably too honest for her own good.

"Did you call Tara and tell her you were heading for the ranch?"

This time Maggie hesitated and they both knew why. Still, she couldn't manage a lie. "Do you have a telephone I could use?"

Curt shook his head, admiring her resourceful way of avoiding lying. "I don't have a phone, but I have a citizen band radio that I use to call the ranch. Do you want me to call Tara?"

Maggie wasn't sure. "How long do you think this storm will last?"

"All night and maybe all day tomorrow."

His guest wasn't pleased to hear his prediction.

"Will it be safe to go to the ranch later if the wind subsides?" Maggie asked.

"Judging the amount of rain we're getting, the road might be impassable for a while."

"Impassable?"

"The culverts weren't built to handle runoff from this heavy a downpour. The road floods deep enough in some spots to drown out a car's engine."

"And the longer it rains, the longer it will take to subside," Maggie surmised grimly.

"Right."

"And it sure doesn't show any sign of stopping, does it?"

"No." His guest would have to spend the night, at least.

"Then I guess there's not much sense in calling the McCains and alarming them."

"No," Curt agreed. "I'll call and tell them I'm staying here, but they don't need to know I have company."

Maggie wondered if she'd be wiser to alert the McCains to her whereabouts. She gave Curt a steady, scrutinizing look that he returned just as steadily.

"The ranch is like a small town," he warned. "If

you hope to work there, it wouldn't be a good idea to let them know you'd spent time alone with me. Even if it is an emergency.''

Maggie understood the logic of his words, but she wasn't totally convinced. There was absolutely nothing she could do if her host decided to violate her trust, yet she still felt the need to offer some sort of protest.

''Do you have a bad reputation with women?''

Her query surprised Curt. Was she so honest that she expected everyone else to be honest and trustworthy? It might do her some good to be a little less trusting, but he wasn't interested in teaching her any lessons.

''Any man who spends the night with a woman can give her a bad reputation, whether she deserves it or not. The ranch staff loves to gossip about anybody and everybody.''

Which didn't exactly answer her question, Maggie thought. Still, what could she do but trust her instincts?

''Maybe you shouldn't mention that I'm here,'' she finally agreed, burying her face in the blanket again.

Curt nodded and headed for his office where he kept the radio.

TWO

Curt's conversation could be heard from the living room. He was telling someone that he was at his ranch and wouldn't try to come any farther tonight. Maggie noticed that although he was succinct, his voice sounded warmer, his southern drawl more pronounced, as though he were talking to someone he really liked.

She realized she wouldn't mind having him talk to her in that tone. The thought was surprising, since she hardly knew the man. She hadn't come to Oklahoma looking for romance.

She was hoping to find an emotionally fulfilling use for a variety of unrelated career skills. In the four years since she'd graduated from college with honors, she hadn't been able to find one occupation or location that had really appealed to her.

Maggie Malone, overachiever, just couldn't seem to settle down anywhere. Chicago was home and she loved to visit, but she didn't like living there. She presently resided in Dallas, but she wasn't happy there, either. Sometimes she thought she was a total misfit and would never find a place where she felt needed for more than her analytical mind and her organizational skills.

Oklahoma and the McCains' ranch was far removed from every other place she'd ever tried to live and work. Maggie was hoping that the drastic change would be a key to success. She was prepared to give it her best shot, should she get hired.

The crackling flames of the fire held her attention while warmth enveloped her and chased away the chills. Her thoughts drifted, and she caught herself dozing. Then the aroma of brewing coffee snapped her back to the present. She loved the smell of coffee. She didn't much care for the taste, but the smell was wonderful.

"Do you take anything in your coffee?" Curt called to her from the kitchen. How had he moved from room to room without her noticing?

"Cream and sugar?" she queried, unsure of his supplies.

"Milk and sugar?" was his response.

"That's fine. Do you need some help?" Maggie offered because her mother had raised a very polite daughter, not because she really wanted to leave her position in front of the fire.

Curt didn't respond. Glancing toward the kitchen, she saw him carrying two mugs of coffee into the room.

Maggie let the blanket drop to her waist as she pulled her arms from the generous folds. She accepted the steaming cup with both hands, giving Curt a smile and a thank you. He took his own cup and sat on the sofa, a few feet from the fireplace.

Cautiously sipping the coffee, Maggie noted that

even the addition of milk and sugar couldn't dilute a brew strong enough to choke a horse. Still, the liquid warmth of the coffee felt good as it slid down her throat. She murmured a sigh of pleasure.

Curt shifted his gaze from the lovely woman sitting in front of his fireplace, but his eyes drifted back to her of their own volition. The firelight was causing red highlights to shimmer in the dark auburn tresses that cloaked her shoulders and fell halfway to her waist.

Her luxurious mass of hair looked too heavy to be supported by such a slender neck. Curt couldn't help wondering what all that silky beauty would feel like in his hands or against his skin. It wasn't wise to speculate, so he forced his eyes back to the dancing flames of the fire.

"My name is Miss Maggie Malone," his guest told him in a faintly mocking tone. "In case you're dying of curiosity."

Miss, that meant trouble. Maggie, he liked. It suited her, but he didn't say so. "I'm not the curious type," was his only comment.

Maggie decided not to be put off by his indifferent attitude. If they were going to spend much time together, she'd go crazy without talking, even if she had to talk to herself.

"Lucky you," she retorted. "My curiosity has gotten me into more than my fair share of trouble."

Just what the McCain ranch needed, Curt thought, an enchanting troublemaker. Maggie's beauty had already convinced him that most of the men within a hundred-mile radius would be fighting for the chance to spend time with her. He frowned in annoyance.

"How long have you been working for the McCains?"

Maggie asked, determined to make the man relax and talk to her.

"About ten years."

"Do you enjoy your work?" She wasn't one to quit until her curiosity was satisfied.

"Yes."

"Do you get along well with the McCains?"

"Yes."

Maggie decided to try another tactic and ask a question that couldn't be answered with one word.

"What does a foreman do on a ranch?"

"Everything." Now Curt's eyes held a glint of challenge. Few people were so persistent when trying to get personal information from him. Nearly everyone of his acquaintance had learned the hard way that he couldn't be prodded, but that he could easily be provoked.

Unfortunately, his guest didn't seem the least bit wary of the challenge in his eyes. Maggie's dark eyes gleamed as they locked with his.

"I told you I have an insatiable curiosity," she reminded softly, without apology.

"And that it got you into a lot of trouble," he recalled, his tone softer than hers but with an undercurrent of steel.

"I never ask for trouble," she supplied while tension vibrated between the two of them with an intensity that was palpable. "But I am known to be irrepressibly optimistic and a bit too strong-willed for my own good. Sometimes the combination leads to trouble."

"Which you don't avoid?"

"Only when the troublesome subject isn't worth the effort."

The question was, did Maggie's interest in her host

stem from idle curiosity or did she think something infinitely more interesting could develop between them?

Curt refused to consider the possibility. He downed his coffee and rose to his feet. "Would you like more coffee?"

Maggie's eyes dropped to her half-full cup and, as usual, she spoke her thoughts. "No, thanks, this should last me for three or four more days."

Curt was already turned toward the kitchen, so Maggie didn't see the amused tilt of his lips. She did watch his easy, graceful stride as he left the room, and sighed softly. The man was definitely a hunk, but he was just as definitely not interested in getting to know her any better.

Maybe he already had a special woman in his life, Maggie thought. Then she wondered why the idea was depressing, even though she'd only just met him. Men like Curt usually had more women than they needed. If they didn't, then they had some serious hang-ups about male-female relationships.

Curt returned to the living room as quietly as he'd left. "I'm going out to my truck. Do you want anything from your car?"

"I have an overnight case in the trunk," Maggie told him, setting her cup on the hearth. "I'll get you my keys."

She started to stand, but her feet were tangled in the blanket and she swayed, losing her balance. Curt was beside her in an instant, clasping her small waist in his big hands, to steady her. Maggie grasped his arms with both hands, but still couldn't get her footing.

Curt shifted a step closer and lifted her straight up in the air so that she could kick her feet free of the blanket.

"Thanks," Maggie told him as she looked bemusedly into his eyes. Her hands were splayed on his upper arms. He'd lifted her one hundred pounds as though she weighed five, and the hard muscles under her palms barely twitched. "You're very strong."

Curt wished she'd be coy and flirtatious. Then he could be disgusted. Instead, her honest observation stroked his ego. "I work hard," was his reply.

Maggie reluctantly broke the contact between them and found her purse. She handed Curt her keys. "It's the blue flight bag."

He turned, and Maggie watched him stride across the room. She willed her pulse to regulate. Physical contact with Curt Hayden, however brief, was a little too unsettling for her normally unshakable calm. She'd never met a man who made her heart trip into overtime at the slightest touch.

Folding the blanket she'd been using kept her busy for a few seconds. Maggie wasn't used to sitting still for long. She stepped into the pumps she'd abandoned earlier and picked up her coffee cup, deciding to get rid of the rest of the gray goo.

She rinsed her mug at the kitchen sink. With the lights on, it was easier to survey her surroundings. This room had obviously been finished for a while. It looked new and rather bare, but all the cabinets were finished and the major appliances had been built into the walls. A stainless steel sink and Formica-topped counter were new, but showed signs of regular use.

There was one table and two chairs. They were solid wood, and she wondered if Curt had made them, too. Both kitchen windows were bare, and Maggie imagined how well her own country print curtains would compliment the beautiful but stark decor.

She heard Curt open the back door and enter the porch, accompanied by the roar of the storm. When he shut the door, the roar lessened again. Maggie hurried to open the kitchen door.

"It doesn't sound like the storm is weakening."

Curt took off his hat and shrugged out of his coat. Then he picked up the bag of groceries he'd collected from his truck.

"It isn't going to let up for a while," he told her as he reached for her bag.

"I can get that," she insisted as she quickly moved to help him.

"It weighs more than you do," Curt said, ignoring her offer to help as he carried everything into the kitchen.

Maggie closed the door behind them. "I don't travel very light," she conceded.

Curt put the groceries on the table, then set her bag inside the living room door. "If you're warm enough now, and hungry, I can fix something to eat."

"I'm warm, thanks, but if you have something else you'd like to do, I'd be happy to fix dinner."

"Supper," Curt corrected.

"Why supper?"

"It's called supper in this part of the country."

Maggie wondered if he was teasing her. "I thought you only called a meal supper if you eat before five o'clock."

"We call it supper whenever we eat."

"Okay," she conceded with a grin. "When in Rome . . ."

Curt didn't return her smile, and she supposed he wanted to show her that a city girl didn't belong in his part of the country. Maybe she didn't, but she had the right to find out for herself.

"I don't keep a lot of food here," Curt told her as he unloaded the bag and put away the groceries.

"I bought a chicken," he added. "I have potatoes and some fresh bread. That will have to do."

"It sounds fine," Maggie replied. "I'll be happy to fry chicken. I can mash potatoes or bake them, whatever you prefer."

"Can you make gravy?" Curt asked, watching her as she began to move around the kitchen, seemingly comfortable with her surroundings.

"It's been a while, but I'll give it a try."

"Then I'd rather have mashed potatoes, if you really don't mind doing the cooking."

"It's your house and your food," she reminded him. "The least I can do is cook for my din—supper."

Curt decided not to argue with her. He never had been fond of cooking. "I have plenty of work to do. Yell if you can't find something you need."

He'd barely turned toward the door when Maggie's hesitant tone halted him.

"Curt?" she said, holding the bag of chicken over the sink and frowning. "It's still whole."

Curt's lips twitched as he joined her at the sink. "She might disagree with you." His tone was lightly amused, with a faint drawl. "She's missing her head and all her feathers."

Maggie rolled her eyes in disgust, but she was delighted by his teasing. "I understand that the poor thing is dead. I wouldn't want to fry her any other way, but it's been years since I saw a whole chicken. I don't think I ever cut one into pieces."

Curt took a sharp knife from a drawer beside the

sink and eased Maggie out of his way. "You can find everything else you need while I cut the chicken."

She didn't argue but moved about the kitchen gathering a skillet, a saucepan, and utensils. She found the potatoes and began peeling them while Curt made short work of the chicken.

"Anything else?" he asked as he washed his hands.

"No, thanks. I think I can find what I need if you don't mind my searching until I learn where everything's kept."

"I don't mind," Curt told her, leaving the kitchen even though he was sorely tempted to stay close to her.

Soon after his departure, Maggie heard music from the other side of the house and realized Curt had switched on a radio. As she busied herself cooking, she heard the occasional sound of an electric power saw and assumed that he was still finishing some construction work.

It wasn't long before the smell of frying chicken permeated the house. Maggie put the potatoes to boil and then set the table. It was obvious from Curt's meager supply of dishes that he didn't do much entertaining.

She didn't know if he'd want coffee for supper, but she decided on milk. There were fresh tomatoes and cucumbers in the refrigerator, so they were sliced and included in her meal plan.

When she wasn't cooking, Maggie poked around the kitchen, looking through drawers, cupboards, and a pantry that was mostly empty. Before long, she'd memorized where every item was stored.

An hour later, they sat down and ate supper in a comfortable silence. Maggie hadn't eaten since breakfast, so everything tasted especially good to her.

Curt was a big man with a healthy appetite. Even

though Maggie had cooked plenty, they ate nearly everything. Two pieces of chicken were all that survived the meal.

"That was good. Thanks for cooking," Curt said when he'd finished his last bite. "I think there's some ice cream in the freezer if you want dessert."

His compliment wasn't lavish, but his tone was warm. It pleased Maggie. "I'm too full right now," she told him. "Would you like me to get you some?" She started to rise.

"You don't have to wait on me," Curt insisted, frowning until Maggie sat down again. "I've had plenty. You can relax while I take care of the dishes."

He rose from his chair and started to clear the table, but Maggie quickly intercepted, taking hold of the dirty plates in his hand. "Go back to your work," she commanded gently, but firmly. "I'll clean the kitchen."

"You did the cooking," Curt argued, his eyes locking with hers as they shared another difference of opinion. He wasn't any more fond of washing dishes than he was of cooking, but he believed in doing his share.

"I don't have anything else to do." Maggie's tone was bland, but her eyes argued sassily with him.

Curt had a feeling she found it hard to do nothing. She reminded him of a hummingbird—small and delicate, yet packed with energy. He let go of the plates.

"I'm working in my office on the other side of the living room. Yell if you need me."

"I will," Maggie promised. "I yell very well."

Curt just nodded and left the room. Maggie noticed that the back of his blue jeans and blue chambray shirt were sprinkled with sawdust. She also noticed how attractively shaped his backside was. Berating herself for such a lascivious thought, she went to work on the dirty dishes.

It was nearing eight o'clock when she finally wandered into the farthest room of the house where Curt was working. A big desk was the only piece of furniture in the office. A shortwave radio was on the desk, along with the AM/FM radio supplying country-western music.

The floor looked finished, but was covered with sawdust. The walls were finished, and an overhead light had been installed. Curt used two sawhorses to support the boards he was cutting.

Maggie watched him measure, mark, and saw the strips of wood, then carry them up the stepladder and nail them into place. He worked as he seemed to do everything, with a powerful, self-assured ease. She was in the room for several minutes before he finally spoke to her.

"You'll get dirty in here."

Maggie laughed softly, looking down at her wrinkled, green shirtwaist dress that had been so neat a few hours ago. "The dress will wash. It's supposed to be permanent press, but I think the rain put some permanent wrinkles in it."

Curt didn't think a few wrinkles detracted from the shapeliness of the dress or the lady wearing it. He went back to work and tried not to be too aware of her presence.

Since he seemed willing to accept her company, Maggie began to ask him questions about what he was doing. Curt patiently explained that he was laying the final covering of boards on the ceiling. He worked as he talked, never really giving her his full attention.

Maggie carefully studied his every movement. He was left-handed, so he did everything the opposite of how she would do it. She watched closely and found him fascinating.

What she called the "efficiency cells" in her brain kicked into gear as she continued to study his work methods. As usual, she thought of simpler ways to accomplish his objective. She decided to lend him some assistance, even though she didn't know anything about carpentry.

"If you want to measure and cut several pieces at a time, I could carry them to you and you wouldn't have to keep climbing up and down the ladder."

Curt stopped what he was doing and stared at her, his eyes accusing. "Can't you just be still for a little while?"

Maggie returned his stare unflinchingly. "I've never been very good at it."

Sighing and shaking his head in resignation, Curt took her up on her offer. He measured and cut boards for the rest of the ceiling. Then he stayed on the ladder and nailed them into place while Maggie brought the boards to him. The only time he needed to climb up and down the ladder was to move it.

They worked in harmony and silence, except when Curt was satisfying her curiosity about some aspect of woodworking. He couldn't remember willingly answering so many questions in his entire life.

The ceiling was finished in half the time he'd thought it would take. After the last nail was hammered, he folded the ladder and took it to the storage closet. When he returned, Maggie was trying to tidy the room.

"Do you have a broom?" she asked, brushing a strand of hair from her face in a gesture that was rapidly becoming familiar to Curt.

"Yes, but you can't use it," he told her flatly.

Maggie arched her brows and propped her hands on her hips in a belligerent stance.

Curt ignored her little show of defiance and started to order her from the room, but was interrupted by a rumbling round of thunder that drowned the sound of music and made the house shudder. Lightning flashed outside the windows and the lights flickered. The radio faded, but then power returned.

"We're lucky we haven't lost power before now," Curt said, looking at Maggie. "You'd better get cleaned up before the electricity goes. I don't have a backup generator. You can have the bathroom while I clean in here."

Maggie didn't argue. She didn't want to sleep in sawdust. Shaking what she could from her hair and dress, she left Curt and collected her overnight bag from the living room. She found the door to the bathroom on the living room wall behind the staircase.

Except for a cupboard door that hadn't been hung, the bathroom was finished. It was large, with all the normal facilities, plus a big, mirrored vanity. She was happy to find that the shelves of the open cupboard were supplied with towels and washcloths.

Maggie took a yellow sweat suit from her case and laid it over a big towel rack. She collected her personal toiletries and then turned to lock the door before undressing. Unfortunately, the door didn't have a lock.

"Great," she muttered in disgust. The idea of stripping and showering in a stranger's house made her wary. Still, she needed to clean the irritating grit from her hair and skin.

"I don't really think Mr. Hayden is likely to accost you," she told her image in the mirror. "He certainly hasn't paid any undo interest in you so far.'' She would just have to take her chances.

After she'd stripped out of her dress and underwear, she folded them neatly and packed them in her bag. She wrapped a huge bath towel around her so that she wouldn't feel so exposed, then brushed the tangles from her hair and removed her makeup.

When she was ready to shower, she pulled the curtain aside, adjusted the fixtures on the bathtub, turned on the tap, and then let out a startled scream.

The scare she received made her pulse race wildly, but she managed to shut the water off again. She was standing with her back against the wall, trying to calm her frayed nerves when Curt threw open the door and shot her a concerned glance.

"What happened?" he demanded, his tone rough.

Maggie fought to quiet her breathing. She clasped her hands protectively over her chest and prayed the towel wouldn't shift. Acute embarrassment caused a deep blush to creep over her face and neck.

"I think something died in your water system," she told the big man who was suddenly invading her personal space and was more alarming than the water.

"Died?" Curt queried. He moved past her to check the bathtub, thinking that some rodent might have crawled through the water pipes into the tub.

"There's nothing here," he stated, his eyes zeroing in on Maggie again. He didn't need this kind of temptation. She was altogether too appealing.

"It's in the water," she explained, battling to regulate her breathing but for a different reason.

"What's in the water?"

"Blood."

"Blood?" Curt growled. "You mean the water is red."

Maggie nodded in affirmation, causing satin tresses to dance over bare shoulders.

Curt's sigh was heavy and he ran his fingers through his hair in agitation. "The water comes from a ground well. There's iron ore in the ground. The sediment is dark orange."

"So you have orange water?" Maggie replied in amazement, her eyes wide and disbelieving. She wasn't that ignorant about life beyond the city. "The water in the kitchen wasn't orange."

Curt turned on the taps of the bathtub again. The dark water was soon flushed from the pipes, and the water became clear. "The orange sediment builds up in the pipes when they're not flushed regularly. I haven't stayed here for a while, so the residue is worse than usual."

Maggie eased from the wall and peeked around Curt's big body. The water looked fine. She watched as he adjusted the temperature, flipped the tap for the shower, then stood aside and pulled the shower curtain closed.

"All right now?" he asked, turning. The narrowed distance between them made them both sharply aware of the intimacy they were sharing, and the risk.

The breathing space in the bathroom diminished and Maggie took a step backward. "I'll be fine, thank you," she told him in a polite, demure tone.

She chose to ignore the sudden, wicked gleam in his eyes. Dealing with her embarrassment was hard enough. She wasn't prepared to cope with the tension that was as thick as the steam rolling from the shower.

"You're absolutely sure?" Curt mocked gently,

thinking she was the most seductively appealing woman he'd ever met. The devilish part of his nature prompted him to give her a slow, sensual appraisal from the rounded curve of her shoulders to her bare toes. She needed a reminder that he was a normal male.

Maggie's temperature rose several degrees. She'd wanted him to relax and be comfortable with her, but not comfortable enough to start challenging her on a physical level.

"Leave!" Her command was clear, if a little shaky. She hated to sound rude and disrespectful—it was his house—but enough was enough. She stepped as far out of his way as possible.

"Yes, ma'am." Curt obeyed immediately. As he closed the door between them, he heard her grumbling about the need for a lock, and he grinned.

He'd never invited a woman to spend a night in his home, and he didn't want this one here now. But his unexpected guest was certainly an intriguing bundle of femininity. She was sassy and sexy, yet sweetly shy.

Her blush had tinted the creamy flesh from her cheeks to the knot in the towel over her breasts. Curt couldn't help but wonder how far the blush continued down the diminutive, but lushly curved body.

Damn! He didn't need a woman in his life, invited or uninvited. He had to exert more control over his imagination and overactive libido.

The lady wouldn't be staying long, he reminded himself. He wouldn't want her to. He never wanted women around for very long.

THREE

Maggie hurried through her shower as quickly as possible. The lights kept flashing, and she didn't want to get caught wet and naked if the electricity failed.

When she was dry, dressed in her sweat suit, and had her damp hair wrapped in a towel, she quickly shoved all her belongings into her bag and vacated the bathroom. She found Curt in the living room and, judging by the cool look he gave her, she didn't have to worry about a repeat of his earlier teasing. His hard, indifferent mask was securely in place.

"I'm finished in the bathroom," she told him, laying her bag beside the sofa and noticing that he'd put the radio, a lantern, and a flashlight on the hearth.

"I think we'll lose the electricity soon," Curt said. "I'm going to take a quick shower. The fireplace will light this room, and you can use the extra lights if you want. The radio operates on batteries."

Maggie nodded, then grabbed for the towel wrapped on her head. She pulled it off and shook her hair free, planning to comb and dry it in front of the fire.

Curt didn't know why the simple action made his blood race, but he decided his shower had better be a cold one.

"Do you have a clothes washer and dryer?" Maggie asked him as he was leaving the room. "I didn't see any, but I wasn't sure if you had a laundry room or a basement."

"The room off the kitchen will be a utility room when I get the wiring done, but I don't have a washer and dryer. Why?"

Maggie realized that the room she'd thought was a huge pantry would be the laundry room. "I thought I might be able to wash a load of towels before the electricity goes off. I always have to use extras for my hair."

Curt was shaking his head in disbelief. She just couldn't stop looking for things to do. "I do my laundry at the other ranch. Don't worry about it." It wasn't a suggestion but a command.

"Okay," Maggie amiably conceded while choosing to ignore his objections. She could bring a chair from the kitchen and dry her towel by the fireplace.

Curt left the room, still shaking his head and knowing her thoughts had already skipped to a satisfactory way to accomplish her objective.

Maggie waited until she heard the shower running, then brought a chair from the kitchen, being careful not to put it too close to the fire. She laid her wet towel over the back and sat down long enough to comb the tangles from her hair.

Her thoughts turned to Curt and the night they would be sharing. Where would they sleep? A quick investigation of the house proved there were no extra rooms downstairs and the rooms upstairs were bare and unfinished.

That left the living room. She wondered if he slept on the sofa, and then guessed that the sofa made into a bed.

Beneath the cushions on the sofa was a handle that pulled the mattress out of the frame. Maggie tossed the cushions on the floor and converted the sofa to a bed. There were two clean sheets tucked in the mattress, so she made the bed and simultaneously decided to make good use of the sofa cushions.

She knew Curt would insist that she take the bed. It wasn't a good idea to share the bed, but she didn't want her host to sleep on the floor. The only solution was to make a second bed on the floor with the sofa cushions. It wouldn't suit his long length, but it would fit her perfectly. Her host wouldn't have a valid argument.

She gave him the blanket she'd snuggled in earlier and stole one of his sheets to wrap around her makeshift mattress. Then she confiscated the second blanket, deciding that she'd done an excellent job of averting any uncomfortable confrontations.

When Curt reentered the living room, he found her sitting comfortably on her makeshift bed, combing her hair as though she'd been doing nothing more than relaxing in front of the fire.

She looked so fragile in her soft yellow sweats with her heavy hair cascading over her shoulders. She looked small and soft and pampered, but she was a miniature dynamo, always two steps ahead in her thinking.

He didn't bother to question her decision to sleep on

the floor. He was sure she had her mental arguments fully prepared.

Maggie let out a tiny sigh of relief when she realized that Curt wasn't going to give her a hard time about their sleeping arrangements. She had just enough time to see how gorgeous he was in clean, faded jeans and a half-buttoned cotton shirt, before the lights flickered for the last time.

They waited, but the electricity didn't surge back to life. Curt moved across the room and lit the oil lantern, keeping the flame low to prevent excessive smoking.

"I guess it's bedtime," Maggie declared, her eyes drifting to Curt's curly-haired chest at the open collar of his shirt. He was close enough for her to smell the clean, masculine scent of him and watch the play of muscles in his long legs as he bent to the lantern.

His blond, sun-streaked hair turned to spun gold in the firelight, and his big body radiated virility. Maggie didn't realize she was holding her breath until he moved away from her again.

Tossing the bath towel to the hearth, Curt moved the chair to the other side of the sofa and used it to hold the lantern off the floor. Between the fireplace and the lantern, the room was softly illuminated.

Maggie had her left side toward the fire and was facing the sofa bed. She was comfortable, but noted that one side of her was going to be much too warm if she stayed so close to the fire.

She squirmed a little, reached for her pocketbook, and put her comb in it. Then she tossed her hair over her shoulders and watched Curt as he moved around the house, flashlight in hand, turning off light switches and locking doors.

"Anything I can do to help?" she asked him as he returned to the living room.

"There's not much to do," Curt replied, shutting off the flashlight and handing it to Maggie. "Keep this by your side in case you need it tonight."

"Thanks," she said, laying the flashlight beside the cushions. Springs squeaked as Curt stretched out on the sofa bed, and her pulse accelerated for some inexplicable reason.

"You can switch the radio to battery operation if you'd like to hear news or music," he said. "There's a button on the right side."

Maggie pulled the radio closer to her and pressed the button. She needed a distraction. The announcer gave the time as eleven o'clock and then followed with five minutes of updated local and national news.

They were both silent and the weatherman promised that tomorrow would bring an end to the rain and a return of summertime temperatures. An unseasonably low temperature was forecast for the remainder of the night.

"It might get cold in here again," Curt predicted, his voice drifting to Maggie from the middle of the sofa. "The furnace thermostat works on an electric control."

"Should I keep adding logs to the fire?" she wanted to know.

"I'll take care of the fire," he told her. "Unless you have a built-in alarm system that wakes you every hour or so." He wouldn't doubt that she did.

Maggie usually slept like a log, but she thought tonight might be an exception. "We can take turns," she compromised.

Curt just grunted.

The two of them grew quiet. The radio station's disk jockey introduced his show as an evening of love songs, and Maggie felt like howling in response. Her senses were already heightened to a fever pitch, and she was far too restless for comfort or sleep.

Flickering firelight cast soft, multicolored shadows around them. Haunting melodies from one love song after another filled the room, the husky, sensual tones enveloping them in a web of intimacy that soon grew too intense to bear.

After half an hour of the slow, painful seduction of her senses, Maggie decided to break the pulsing silence.

"I've never listened to country-western music before," she told Curt, whether he wanted to hear or not.

"Never?" His disbelief was obvious.

"I've heard a lot of songs that bridge the gap between country and contemporary, but I've never heard so many different songs." Maggie was a little surprised by her admission. She considered herself a music lover, yet for years she'd been ignorant of a whole category of beautiful songs with poignant lyrics.

"I suppose you're a classical music lover," Curt said.

"I like classical music," Maggie defended, shifting her right side to the fire and cooling her left. "Especially if I can hear it at a live concert, but I like a lot of other styles of music, too."

"Heavy metal?"

"Well," she hedged, shifting onto her back. "I like a few heavy metal songs, but mostly just the rhythm. I can't ever make sense of the lyrics."

"I didn't know they had lyrics."

Maggie shifted onto her side again. "I think they're

written in a futuristic language," she supplied, and shifted once again.

"How do you ever get to sleep if you can't lay still for two minutes?" Curt asked, her restlessness making him restless.

"I'm just not sleepy," Maggie explained. "It really isn't very late. I don't suppose you'd like to dance?"

"I don't think that would be a very good idea," Curt responded in a low, soft drawl. His body was already taut from imagining what she'd feel like in his arms, he didn't need proof.

"No, I don't suppose it would be too wise." Maggie silently agreed that the tension between them was potentially explosive. The impulsive part of her nature wanted to investigate the increasing attraction she felt for the big cowboy. Another part of her—the practical, sensible part—told her the risk was too great.

The next song on the radio was slow and suggestive, about a woman who wanted to be treated like a stranger. She wanted her lover to pretend they'd just met and fallen in love all over again. Maggie squirmed.

Then came a husky baritone singing about making love with slow hands. The next song was a tribute to a wonderful lover. The singer wasn't the least shy about expressing his desires. Maggie turned over, settling on her stomach with her chin propped on her hand.

Her voice was a little husky as she spoke in the direction of the sofa. "My grandmother would call your music 'earthy.' She always uses that word instead of 'sexy.' I suppose it has to do with proper etiquette."

"I don't want to talk about sexy." Curt's tone was firm but gruff.

"How about my grandmother?" Maggie teased, pleased that he was as uncomfortable as she.

"How about being still and going to sleep?"

She sighed dramatically and laid her head down, but she wasn't used to sleeping without a pillow. Searching for a substitute, she eyed the towel Curt had tossed to the floor.

She started to pull it toward her and caught sight of something moving on the floor. An ugly, hairy black spider scurried in one direction, and Maggie scurried in the opposite, choking back a squeal of alarm.

"What is it?" Curt was off the sofa in an instant.

"Nothing, really," she insisted, calming herself. "It was just a spider. It startled me, but I think I scared it just as badly."

"Probably," Curt agreed. He picked up the flashlight and checked the area around her bed, but the spider was long gone. "Why don't you take the sofa?"

"No," Maggie argued, stretching along the cushions and pulling the blanket over her. "I'm fine right here. Besides, that old spider could climb right up on the bed if he wanted."

Curt's grin was lost in the darkness as he shut off the flashlight, turned off the lantern, and added another log to the fire. When he straightened to return to bed, he found Maggie's eyes watching him.

Stretched out in the firelight, she was incredibly lovely and more alluring than any women he'd ever tried to resist. Her hair was glorious, her eyes darkly shadowed, and the blanket did little to disguise her lovely form.

Tension crackled like the flames of the fire. Maggie was suddenly too hot all over. No amount of shifting was going to make it better.

Curt dampened his desire with difficulty. It had been a long time since he'd been with a woman, but he was used to weeks of celibacy. The ache would subside eventually.

"Do you want me to turn the radio off?" he asked Maggie.

"It doesn't matter to me," she replied a bit huskily. "I'm going to lie still and be quiet as a mouse. . . ." As soon as the words were out of her mouth, she began to squirm, wishing she hadn't thought of mice.

Her sudden anxiety broke the tension between them. She heard the amusement in Curt's tone when he tried to reassure her. "I built this house myself. There's not a pinhole big enough for a mouse to get through."

"I'm very relieved to hear that," Maggie clipped, tucking the blanket around her in mummy fashion, hoping to keep any sort of creepy crawlies from getting too close to her.

Curt turned the radio off and stretched out on the sofa bed again. The room grew quiet, and he forced himself to think of things that were unrelated to women and sex—especially sexy little women with sharp minds and soft bodies.

Maggie couldn't quite forget about spiders and mice. She decided that she'd wait until Curt was asleep and then bring the other chair from the kitchen. She'd rather sleep sitting up than share her bed with uninvited guests.

The room was growing cool, and she slowly kept turning one side of her body, then the other, toward the fire. She listened until Curt's breathing had been soft and steady for about fifteen minutes, then she turned on the flashlight and quietly brought another chair from the kitchen.

After placing the lantern on the floor, Maggie put both chairs in front of the fireplace, facing one another.

She added another log to the fire and wrapped her blanket around her, Indian fashion. Then she sat in one chair, and propped her legs up on the other. At first, it wasn't too uncomfortable.

Unfortunately, it became very uncomfortable and very, very cold. Maggie didn't want to risk moving the chairs too close to the fire, but she couldn't do much shifting in her present position.

It had been a long day, and she was exhausted. She needed to get some sleep before her job interview with the McCains. Otherwise, she'd look and sound like a complete zombie.

Folding a corner of the blanket and tucking it behind her neck, she cushioned her head, and tried not to think about how cold she was getting. The fire was still crackling, so she turned her face toward its heat, and eventually drifted to sleep.

Curt was exhausted, too. He rested quietly, but hadn't allowed himself to fall asleep while Maggie was still roaming around the house. He listened to her movements and smiled slightly when he realized that she was moving off the floor. When she finally settled and slept, he did, too.

It was much later when Curt awakened to the realization that the room was very cold. It was still dark and the fire had faded to bright ashes. He rose, tossed a couple of logs on it and turned to Maggie.

She'd abandoned the chairs and was curled in a tight ball on the floor in her makeshift bed. Knowing he'd be sorry, but too cold and tired to care, he scooped her small body into his arms and carried her to his bed.

Maggie moaned and wrestled with him when he took her blanket, but quieted when he pulled her close and threw both blankets over them. She snuggled closer to the warmth of his body with a shiver and a soft sigh.

Curt wrapped his arms around her, stroking her gently until the shivering subsided. Maggie gradually relaxed in his arms, murmuring huskily and molding her small, shapely frame to fit the hard angles of his. Curt felt her softness, inhaled the sweetness of her scent, and ordered himself to go back to sleep.

It was the most incredible dream. Maggie had never felt so safe and secure. The man in her dream had no face and no name, but her heart knew and trusted him. He was lavishing her with tenderness.

The dream wasn't sexual, but incredibly sensual. Every nerve ending in her body was responding to the feel of the big, warm man. Her breasts were highly sensitized by the friction of contact with a hard chest. Her limbs were heavy from arousal, and a sweet ache was intensifying deep within her.

His arms protected her and she sighed with satisfaction. She'd found a place where she was needed. The man in her dreams made her feel wanted and loved. She finally knew where she belonged and how it felt to fit so perfectly in a man's arms, as if they'd been made especially for her.

Maggie knew she was waking from her dream, but she clung to the last remnants of sleep. She wanted to know more about her dream man. She wanted more time with him. She didn't want to wake up and be cold again.

Her soft moans and warm breath were whispering against Curt's chest, teasing one nipple to a rigid peak of hardness. It wasn't the only part of his body that ached with hardness. Every inch of him was hard and throbbing. He couldn't remember ever fighting such a hellish battle with his own desires.

He'd slept for a couple of hours, then awakened to find himself literally wrapped around Maggie. His arms were locked about her slender body and his legs were tangled with hers. Her face was pressed against his chest. One of her arms was around his waist and the other was trapped between their bodies, her hand brushing against the most rigid part of his anatomy.

Curt knew he should have untangled himself and gotten out of bed as soon as he woke, but he hadn't. He'd continued to hold his uninvited guest and enjoy the pleasure-pain of feeling her small body snuggled close to his.

She wasn't his type at all. He didn't have much to do with women, but when he did, he wanted them tough, experienced, and emotionally detached. He didn't want or need sweetness. He didn't want inquisitive and challenging and sassy as hell. He didn't want the type of woman who expected too much, because he didn't have that much to give.

What he wanted was her sexy body. That's all, he argued silently. He just wanted to bury himself in her softness and satisfy the ache in his loins. He wanted to suckle the nipples that were tight little beads against his chest. He wanted to see all of the lovely body that felt so good against him.

He wanted to feel her silky hair against his naked flesh. They both had on too many clothes. He wanted them out of the way. He wanted to explore every inch of her petite body. He wanted her small, soft hands all over him, and maybe even her sassy little mouth.

Curt's hips arched involuntarily, rubbing against Maggie's hand and causing another surge of arousal.

His moan was low and tortured as blood roared through his body and the aching intensified. He briefly considered seducing her as she awakened, satiating himself with her exquisite body, and then forgetting about it.

Maggie's long lashes drifted open as she reluctantly awoke from her incredibly erotic dream. For just a few seconds, dream and reality mingled as she tilted her head backward and looked into Curt Hayden's passion-clouded blue eyes.

Closing her eyes again, she admonished herself for giving her dream man a face and a name. It had just been a dream. There was no passionate man in her life and never had been. Men treated her like a cute little girl, not like the sensuous woman she was. Curt Hayden barely tolerated her.

Then whose big, hard body was enveloping hers? Maggie wondered, her eyes widening as she came more fully awake. This time when her eyes met Curt's, she recognized the hunger in his. She was amazed, yet not alarmed.

"Good morning," she said with a shy smile, trying to collect her sleep-scattered thoughts.

The husky greeting nearly shattered Curt's control. His arms tightened, crushing every inch of her soft body against his hard one. He didn't try to return her greeting.

The intimacy of their position gradually dawned on Maggie. She was completely locked against Curt's very hard, very male body. Her legs were tucked between his thighs, her breasts pressing deeply against his chest with every breath. One of her hands was cradling the rigid evidence of his arousal.

How the hell had this happened? Had she climbed into bed with the man and thrown herself at him?

"I was having this dream," Maggie tried to explain. "I was so cold and then so wonderfully warm."

Curt's voice was a little hoarse when he spoke. "You were freezing on the floor and I put you in bed with me."

That was a relief. Maggie was glad she hadn't climbed into his bed uninvited. Now she just had to figure a way to get out of it without creating any physical friction.

Curt noticed that she was holding herself perfectly still, hardly moving a muscle. He wondered if she was alarmed by his blatant arousal. If she'd slept with many men, she must know that it was a perfectly normal reaction.

He shifted his hips and Maggie gasped softly, then tried to pull her hand from between their bodies. Her eyes flew to Curt's and the flush in her cheeks deepened.

"Am I shocking you?" he asked, his tone huskily amused.

"Of course not." It was just a white lie. The truth was, she liked the feel of him a little too much, but she wasn't quite bold enough to say so.

"Do you sleep with many men?" he asked, shocking her with the first personal question he'd asked.

"None," Maggie retorted baldly. When he decided to get personal, he was remarkably blunt. "Not that it's any of your business."

"You're right," he drawled softly, his eyes locking with hers. "It's not my business, but I didn't want to make any more moves that might shock you."

Maggie silently cursed the blush that just grew hotter.

Curt wondered how far the blush spread over her breasts.

Maggie wondered how she was going to untangle herself without rubbing him the wrong way.

Curt wished she would rub him a little harder.

"How should we do this?" she finally managed. "Should we do it slow and easy or fast and hard?"

A tremor shot through Curt and Maggie found herself stuttering. "I . . . I meant how should we get out of bed. Our arms and legs will be numb and will sting like crazy. Should we move slowly or very quickly, like removing a Band-Aid?"

"I always hated having Band-Aids ripped off me," Curt growled, sliding his face over her silky, sweet-smelling hair.

He didn't seem to be in a big hurry to release her, and Maggie fought the urge to encourage his attentions. They were both highly aroused and there would be no crime in exploring the attraction between them, yet she wasn't used to casual sex.

Curt hadn't done or said anything since meeting her that suggested he even liked her. She was learning to like him altogether too much, but she wasn't interested in a one-sided love affair. She wasn't interested in a love affair at all.

"We really should get out of bed," she murmured quietly, her face close to the tight blond curls at the open neck of his shirt. She couldn't remember ever being so tempted to make love with someone she'd only known for hours. She just wasn't the type to throw caution to the wind.

Curt knew she was right. Even if they were both consenting adults, it was a bad idea to get any more involved. He didn't like involvement. If Maggie took the job at the ranch, they'd be working together occasionally, and things could get complicated. He tried to dampen his rampaging desire.

She was trying, too, but she couldn't put any distance between their aroused bodies until Curt eased his hold on her. Her dark eyes beseeched him to make the first move.

Slowly, with obvious reluctance, he released her and stretched his long length beside her shorter one. Closing his eyes, he sighed heavily and willed away the tension.

Maggie groaned when her arms and legs painfully regained their circulation. "Damn!" she groused, briskly shaking her arms, then rubbing her legs to minimize the stinging.

Her swearing made Curt's lips twist derisively. *Damn* was mild compared to how he was feeling. The return of circulation wasn't half as painful as the unsatisfied desire.

He'd known this woman was going to be trouble since the first instant he laid eyes on her. What he hadn't expected was that he'd be asking for trouble. He normally didn't get involved with women, especially strangers.

When he wanted sex, he saw someone who provided it without complications. He needed to stick to his usual habits and avoid contact with pint-sized packages of trouble. It was time to get her out of his house and out from under his skin.

He got out of the bed and left the room.

FOUR

When Maggie heard the shower running, she started straightening the room: changing the bed into a sofa and folding sheets and blankets. She carried the chairs back to the kitchen and tidied the living room.

Next she brushed her hair and fastened it with a barrette at the nape of her neck. There wasn't much she could do about her wrinkled clothing until Curt was finished in the bathroom, so she went in search of food.

There were eggs in the refrigerator, so Maggie decided to fry eggs and make toast. She didn't know if Curt was used to a big breakfast, but judging by the size of last night's meal, he probably needing feeding three times a day.

She read the instructions on a can of coffee, then doubled the amount of grounds, hoping her brew would be strong enough to satisfy her host.

All the time she was working, Maggie tried to keep memories of the night from her thoughts. Normally, if she concentrated on every little thing she did, she could

53

block all other thoughts from her mind. It wasn't working this morning.

Visions of Curt kept flashing to the front of her mind. She couldn't manage to banish the memory of his hungry eyes and aroused body. He was very much a man, and she was almost sorry she hadn't taken advantage of the only chance she'd probably ever get to know his loving. She knew his detached demeanor would be back in place, probably reinforced by this morning's intimacy.

The warm, erotic feelings she'd experienced while dreaming kept nagging at her subconscious. Wild excitement and the memory of the desire she'd sparked made her ache for something that she couldn't even put a name to.

She'd never had much experience with men on a passionate level. Mostly she got bored with them before their relationship had time to develop beyond friendship. Men she'd considered good friends had treated her like a kid sister. Her one experience with sex had left her totally disgusted.

Curt Hayden was a new and unique challenge to her senses. Maggie had never known such incredible temptation. She'd never been so aroused or thought it possible to desire someone on such a short acquaintance.

She'd always thought that desire gradually developed from long-established relationships. She hadn't thought she could physically want someone who wasn't emotionally involved with her. She wasn't stupid enough to think that everyone who shared sex was emotionally committed to his partner, but she had thought it would be of the utmost importance to her.

Maggie set the table, started cooking the eggs, and put bread in the toaster. The shower shut off, and she knew Curt would soon be ready to eat. She wondered if they would find each other as appealing in the cold light of day.

As Curt left the bathroom he simultaneously smelled coffee brewing and noted that Maggie had already cleaned the living room. Now she was busy cooking breakfast.

He couldn't help but wonder about having all that energy channeled to passion. Despite a cold shower, his body began to harden again at the thought.

The fuse on his temper was getting shorter by the minute. He wasn't angry with Maggie for being so sexy and sensual, but he was furious with himself for wanting her more than he'd ever wanted anything in his life.

And he couldn't have her—not today, not ever. Not even if she was eager and willing. Making love to her would be a mistake, a serious mistake that he couldn't afford to make. He didn't have the capacity for emotions that women like Maggie always wanted and needed, maybe even deserved.

"You didn't have to cook breakfast," Curt told her as he entered the kitchen, heading straight for the coffeepot.

Maggie took one look at him and knew the feelings she'd been battling weren't temporary or likely to disappear. She almost groaned at her body's instant reaction to his presence. He was so solid, sexy, and virile. His jeans and shirt were worn and faded, so they clung like a second skin, molding his gorgeous physique and reminding her of how that body felt against hers.

"I don't mind cooking," she replied, turning her eyes back to the skillet on the stove. "I'm frying the eggs—is that okay?"

"Fine," Curt said, then asked, "do you want me to pour your coffee?"

"No, thanks," she responded quickly. "I don't drink much coffee."

"No slave to caffeine?" he asked as he carried his cup to the table and sat down.

"I'm addicted," Maggie told him lightly, "but I get my high from tea and cola."

"Sorry about that. I don't have either."

"I'll survive," Maggie told him as she carried their plates to the table and sat down. "I like milk, too." She was having milk this morning.

The small talk ceased so that they could eat while their food was hot. They ate automatically, but neither of them really tasted the food.

Curt was too aware of her presence: of her beauty and of her sweetness. When he was close to her, his senses were seduced and refused to respond to mental commands.

Maggie was relieved that Curt even spoke to her. She knew he didn't want her in his house, and she knew she'd caused him considerable sexual frustration. She was glad she hadn't totally alienated him and hoped they could part amiably.

"It looks like summer has returned," Maggie commented when they'd both finished eating.

Curt glanced out the window. It was early, but the sun was shining brightly, and the wind had subsided.

"It won't take long for the ground to absorb the extra rain," he told her.

Maggie took that as a hint that she should be on her way. Rising from her chair, she started to clear the table, but one of Curt's big hands closed over hers.

"Don't even think about it," he growled, making her release the dirty plate. Their eyes locked for an instant and then quickly shifted. "I'll clean the kitchen this morning. Have another glass of milk."

"If you're going to do the dishes, I'll take a turn at the bathroom," she told him as she rose and carefully eased past him to the doorway.

Curt just nodded and started carrying dishes to the sink.

Maggie grabbed her flight bag and headed toward the bathroom.

She didn't shower because she didn't want to get her hair wet or get naked again in Curt's house. She bathed from the sink, brushed her teeth, and twisted her hair into a chignon. Then she changed her sweat suit for a pair of slightly wrinkled gray knit slacks and a pale blue blouse.

The outfit would be all right this morning, but she would have to return to Larson, find a motel room, and iron another dress before her interview. She didn't want to go straight to the McCain ranch from here. She needed time to reorganize her thoughts and reestablish some measure of professionalism.

Maggie tidied the bathroom and made sure she had all of her belongings packed in her bag. She carried it into the living room and put it by the sofa, then steadied herself to return to the kitchen.

Curt had his back to her, but knew the instant she entered the room. He could hear her, feel her, smell her. She'd be leaving soon and there'd be no more shared intimacy. He knew he should be pleased. He wasn't, and that irritated him.

Maggie was at a temporary loss for words and actions. Curt Hayden had an amazing effect on her. She had no experience dealing with a lack of conversation and activity. A glance at her watch prompted words.

"It's nearly eight o'clock. Do you think the roads will be safe now?"

Curt turned to her, eyes narrowing at the glimmer of reluctance he saw in her eyes. He didn't want to care about her feelings. He didn't even want to recognize the shy hesitancy.

"Are you going to the ranch now?" he asked as he slowly narrowed the distance between them.

Maggie shook her head. For some reason her mouth went dry and her pulse skipped a beat. She swallowed and explained. "I'm going back to Larson."

"You've changed your mind about working for the McCains?"

Curt's voice had an edge to it, and Maggie wasn't sure whether he wanted her to honor her commitment to the McCains or just go away. "I'm still interested in the job. I just want to wait until this afternoon before I go to the ranch."

He seemed to relax a little at her explanation. Maggie stood perfectly still in the kitchen doorway. She knew one of them should break the increasing tension between them, but she didn't know how to do it. She didn't realize that her eyes were beseeching Curt to do or say something that would assure her he wasn't sorry he'd rescued her from the storm.

Curt's eyes became tangled with hers, and his whole body went taut. She was so incredibly lovely. Her dark eyes seemed to reach into his soul and touch him in places he'd never allowed another person to touch.

His thoughts were churning. She was a serious threat to his peace of mind, and he'd fought long and hard for that peace. Wanting her was dangerous. Letting her want him was wrong.

He knew he had to destroy what was growing between them, but he didn't know how to do it painlessly.

"I'll carry your bag to the car," Curt finally broke the heavy silence.

He started around Maggie, and she tried to shift out of his way but managed to shift the same way he did. They both moved the other direction at the same time. Then Curt's hands came up and locked on her arms. He'd planned to move her out of his way, but when her hands flattened against his chest, he felt a jolt of fire scorch his skin.

Maggie was amazed yet again by the hard warmth of his body. She started to withdraw her touch, but her actions were as slow as a caress. "You're so hard," she told him, tilting her head to look into his stormy eyes.

She moved her hands across his chest to his shoulders and down his arms. "Every inch of you is as hard as rock," she continued lightly with disarming fascination.

Curt's grip on her arms tightened and he pulled her closer, his tone going low and gruff with warning. "The hardness goes all the way to the heart. It's not just surface. I don't have one ounce of softness to give anyone."

Maggie's eyes widened as she studied the stony features of his handsome face. His jaws were rigid with control. His eyes glinted with warning. He didn't want her getting any ideas about the two of them. He was making it clear that he didn't feel anything at all for her.

"You can't deny there's a strong attraction," she breathed softly.

"Physically, we'd be dynamite together," Curt drawled softly, watching her eyes dilate as he felt the familiar tightness in his loins. "But pretty little ladies are never satisfied with just sex."

"Sex is all you're interested in?" Maggie wanted him to convince her. "If sex was all you wanted, you could have taken advantage of my vulnerability last night or this morning. We both know I wouldn't have offered much objection."

Hearing her admit that she wanted him made Curt's blood throb painfully through his body. He had to discourage her from reading too much into his restraint. The only convincing way to reject her innocent overtures was with brutal honesty.

His arms tightened around her and lifted her tightly against him so that she could feel the strength of his arousal. He determinedly blocked out his own swift, hot reaction to having her close.

"I wanted your body last night, this morning, even now. The male in me wants a female to relieve the ache. Any female would do."

"I'm female." Maggie's breathless challenge fell on the thick tension between them. "Why didn't you use me to ease the ache?"

Curt growled, a very male, very aroused growl. A tremor shuddered over his body and his arms tightened painfully about her slight form. "Because I want it hard and fast, lady," he snarled, his tone deliberately ugly.

"The way I want you would rip your sweet body apart. I like my women as hard as I am. There's no room in my life for softness."

Fire shot through Maggie, and she trembled but not from fear. She knew he was trying to scare her, but how could she believe the tough-guy act after the way he'd held her? She was trembling so hard that she didn't try to speak, but her eyes called him a liar.

Curt snarled at her, and his arms tightened bruisingly, forcing her body so tightly against his that neither could catch their breath. Then he brought his mouth down hard on her trembling lips. It wasn't a kiss but a brutal punishment for her sassy refusal to heed his warning.

Maggie's head was forced backward until she thought her neck would snap. The cruel, insulting pressure of Curt's mouth ground her lips against her teeth with a violence that was totally alien. She couldn't breathe, and she was on the verge of passing out when he finally released her.

Maggie swayed dizzily, but Curt's arms steadied her, contradicting his attempt to prove how ruthless and uncaring he was. Grasping the door frame for balance, she pulled from his hands and speared him with wide, wounded eyes.

"You've made your point," she told him, the strength gradually returning to her voice. "I hadn't realized I was making such a nuisance of myself. I apologize for invading your privacy. I won't make the mistake again."

Curt pushed past her without a word. He collected her case from the living room and left the house without giving her another glance.

When Maggie's legs had stopped trembling, she went to the living room and rummaged in her purse until she found two twenty-dollar bills. She tossed them on the sofa in payment for a night's food and lodging. Then she followed Curt outside.

Neither of them spoke as Maggie climbed into her car and started the engine. She didn't even glance back as she left his driveway and turned toward town.

Curt watched her go, making sure she headed in the

right direction. His eyes were focused on the sports car, but all he could see were her big, wounded brown eyes. Damn! Women!

They always wanted more than he was capable of giving. They always acted shattered when they learned that his emotions didn't run deep. He'd spent a lifetime hardening himself to emotion of any kind. Still, the women always shackled him with the guilt.

Much later that day, Maggie drove past Curt's ranch on her way to the McCains'. She was engulfed by sadness, but forced herself to concentrate on her interview.

She knew the McCains wanted a secretary who was good with computers and was willing to live on the ranch. She didn't know anything about ranch life, but she could learn, providing they were willing to take the time to train her.

The huge iron gates and security check were impressive. Maggie found the sight of the ranch house and property equally impressive. Everything showed signs of quality care and upkeep. She was happy to see that her prospective employers had pride in their operation and the good sense to take care of it.

After parking beside a candy–apple red Porsche, Maggie grabbed her purse and stepped from the car, then smoothed the skirt of her navy suit. She climbed the steps to the porch and knocked on the front door. Her smile grew a little stiff at the first sight of a big, gorgeous stranger who opened the door.

"You must be Maggie Malone," the man said, waving her into the house. "I'm Rand McCain. My wife is waiting in the office for us."

Maggie wondered if all the men in Oklahoma were big, hard, and handsome. His golden hair and brilliant green eyes made her prospective employer a real knock-out. She groaned inwardly at the thought. Great-looking men usually had oversize egos. She hoped Rand McCain would be different.

Tara McCain rose from her seat at the computer as Rand and Maggie entered the room. She had dark, curly hair and warm hazel eyes. She introduced herself, insisted that they all be seated, and smiled the warmest welcome Maggie had seen in a long time. The two of them were going to be friends.

"Did you have any trouble finding us?" Tara asked.

"Not really," Maggie replied. "I found Larson without problems, and then stopped at a store for directions."

"I can't tell you how happy we are that you were willing to come to the ranch for an interview," Tara told her. "We've been advertising for a secretary for months, but most people want to move to the city, not from it."

"I've been in a lot of cities," Maggie explained. "I was raised in Chicago, and I've lived in New York, San Francisco, and Boston. I'm currently living in Dallas, but none of those cities has held enough appeal to keep me for more than a year."

"I called your last three employers," Rand told her, his attitude direct. "They were all sorry to lose you. We have no doubt that you're capable of doing the work we need done, but our concern is whether you'll be satisfied to work here for more than a few months."

"I'm expecting a baby in January," Tara explained. "And we have a four-year-old daughter, so Rand wants to make sure we have someone to trust with the business for at least the next year. According to your employment record, that's the longest you've ever stayed in one position, regardless of generous incentives offered by employers.''

Maggie's smile was self-derisive. Her work record was impressive, but her tenure in each position was brief. She always hoped that each new job would provide what was lacking in her life, but so far they had not.

"I can't argue with the facts," Maggie told them. "And I can't promise that I'll be perfect for the job, or that it's perfect for me. I can promise to work hard, and I'm willing to sign a contract with the stipulation that I wouldn't leave until a satisfactory replacement was found, hired, and trained.

"The truth is, I left most of my other positions because I'm an efficiency expert. Sometimes I organize myself right out of a job. In Dallas, my employer wanted to keep me on staff, but there was very little actual work to be done, and I can't stand being idle. I'm rather a misfit, and I'm hoping that working on a ranch might offer some totally different challenges."

Tara laughed out loud, and Rand grinned. The smile they exchanged was an approval of her candor.

"I promise you the ranch will offer constant challenges," Tara said. "I've had some experience in the business world, and the ranching business incorporates a lot of the same challenges as well as a million unrelated ones. I don't think you'll ever have to worry about getting idle or bored around here."

Her declaration brought a wide smile to Maggie's lips and enthusiasm to her bright eyes. "Those are sweet words. I'm not really a nomad by nature, I'm sure of it, yet I haven't found any job that can satisfy my need for activity without boring me to death. My mother says that God may have shorted me in the size department, but he gave me a double dose of energy.''

Tara laughed again, and Maggie noted that Rand's eyes sparkled at the sound of her laughter. She breathed a silent sigh of relief, realizing she wouldn't have to worry about unwanted overtures from this handsome employer. He didn't try to disguise his adoration of his wife.

"Maggie Malone," Rand said, turning eyes on her. "If you want the job, you've got it. The salary is negotiable and you'll have room and board, as well. We prefer you live here so that you're close in case of an emergency. If you have any objection to the lodging, we're willing to consider alternatives.''

"I have no objections," Maggie told him. "It will save me a lot of time and trouble, not to mention monthly utility and grocery bills.''

"Just one warning," Tara added. "You'll officially be a ranch secretary, but more of an assistant with varied duties. We want someone we can depend on. Whether it's for office work, running errands, or just someone who isn't afraid to pitch in and help wherever we need help.

"I know that's asking a lot, but we're willing to pay you well, and you said you didn't mind the variety. If you ever feel like you're being taken advantage of or you aren't getting enough free time, just start yelling.''

Maggie grinned. "It sounds fine. I have a thirst for knowledge that has made some of my employers and co-workers uncomfortable, because I'm never satisfied until I understand everything about every project.''

"Then you wouldn't mind working outside the office on occasion?'' Rand asked.

"Not at all, and I don't particularly want a nine to

five job. I can cook, clean, and even baby-sit. I'm happier when I'm not limited to secretarial duties.''

"Everyone on the ranch has a job classification," Rand explained. "But most of the time we all pitch in and get the work done. Sometimes the business end of the ranching is the most pressing, sometimes it's the actual ranch operations.''

"Well, I don't have any experience in ranching, so I'll have a lot to learn, but I'm not hesitant about trying."

"Great!" Tara exclaimed, rising from her chair. "If you have time right now, we'd like to introduce you to some of the staff. You can start working whenever it's convenient."

"The sooner, the better," Rand injected.

Maggie rose and offered her hand to Tara, and then Rand. "We have a deal. I'm ready to start as soon as I finalize some moving plans. My lease in Dallas expires next week, so all I have to worry about are personal belongings."

"Do you think you'll need a couple weeks or a couple days?" Rand wanted to know.

"A few days should be enough," Maggie replied. "I can be ready to start work early next week, if you'd like."

"I'd like," Rand insisted with emphasis. "Tara hasn't been feeling too well and she needs to get more rest."

"Today's Thursday, and September ends next Monday, so we'll add you to our payroll the first of October. You can start as soon as you get moved," Tara said, turning toward the door.

Maggie agreed and followed her from the office.

Rand moved down the hallway with them and opened the front door.

"Do you have time to meet a few of the staff?"

"Sure," Maggie told her. "I don't have any schedule to adhere to at the moment."

They stepped off the porch and halted briefly while Maggie put her purse in her car. Then they rounded the corner of the house and headed toward the barns, discussing some of the unusual chores that cropped up from time to time.

Summer had returned with a warm breeze and brilliant sunshine. Maggie's hair was loose around her shoulders and she lifted her face to the breeze, inhaling the clean, fresh air.

"There's one thing I should tell you before we meet everyone," she said. "I didn't pick your ranch out of the blue. I have a cousin who works here, so I'd heard a lot of good things about your operation before I decided to apply for the job."

"A cousin?" Rand repeated.

"Who? Why didn't you mention it earlier?" Tara asked.

"I didn't want my relationship with Mike to effect your decision in any way."

"Mike? You're Mike's cousin? That's terrific!" Tara declared as they drew closer to the barns and caught sight of the man in question.

Mike Craton and Curt Hayden, the two ranch foremen, were engrossed in conversation. Rand, Tara, and Maggie were within a few yards of them before being noticed.

Maggie's eyes sought her cousin, shifted to the man beside him, then quickly back to Mike. Curt's hard features didn't invite friendliness. Mike's eyes widened in recognition, amazement, then delight.

"Did Mike know you were applying for the job?" Rand asked.

"No," responded Maggie.

"Midget!" Mike's deep baritone rumbled with surprise and affection as his eyes homed in on Maggie. "Maggie Midget Malone, as I live and breathe!"

When the big, bearlike man came running at the trio Rand and Tara stepped aside. Maggie stepped forward and was swept into his arms.

"What are you doing here?" Mike demanded, effortlessly lifting her off her feet, twirling her around and around as he had done since she was a toddler. "Boy, are you a sight for sore eyes. You get more beautiful every time I lay eyes on you!"

Maggie hugged him fiercely; he'd been her best friend all her life, and she'd missed him. She grasped his wild, dark beard in her hands and held him still while scattering kisses over his forehead and cheeks.

"Hi, big guy. I've been missin' you!" she told him, her eyes sparkling with love and laughter.

"You must really be missin' me if you drove all the way out here to say hi," Mike insisted, setting her on her feet again and giving her a smacking kiss on the forehead.

"I hate to burst your bubble," Tara teased, "but she's here for more than a visit with you."

Mike's dark eyes met Maggie's. "What's happening?"

"I've just accepted a job as ranch secretary."

"No kidding?" Mike roared in amazement, his eyes flying to Rand for confirmation. At his boss's affirmative nod, he shook his head in frustration.

"Why didn't you tell me you were thinking about changing jobs? I could have—"

Maggie stilled his words with a hand over his mouth. "I know you would have done your best to see that I got the job if I wanted it," she told him with a cheeky grin.

"But you're so damned independent that you had to do it all by yourself, right?" Mike demanded with a mock growl.

"It's the best way," countered Maggie, giving Rand and Tara a grin. "Besides, how was I to know if your recommendation would be favorable?"

The McCains chuckled, and Mike growled at her again. "You little minx, I'll have to teach you some manners while you're here. I can see you've forgotten your proper little lady manners."

His words instantly reminded Maggie of Curt. She shot the other man a glance and found his eyes locked on her, nearly searing her with their heat. He looked furious for an instant, and then regained his steely countenance.

The brief voltage of highly charged emotion caused Maggie's pulse to quicken. If she didn't know better, she'd swear he looked jealous, not just angry at having to see her again.

"Curt, come meet the light of my life, and the new ranch secretary," Mike insisted, turning to allow Maggie an unblocked view of him. "At least, I assume she's been hired," he teased.

Rand assured him that she was taking the job. Curt moved closer, and Maggie's stomach muscles tightened, her throat going dry. Don't act like a lovestruck teenager, she admonished herself, and managed a weak smile.

FIVE

"Curt Hayden, Maggie Malone," Tara made the introductions.

Curt nodded a greeting. Maggie offered a hand, but regretted the action when his touch sent a bolt of lightning shooting up her arm. They were quick to end the contact.

"Curt and Mike share the ranch management," Rand explained. "They're my left and right hands. With a place this size, it takes all three of us to keep up with the work."

"How big is your ranch?" Maggie asked, trying to calm her racing pulse and appear normal. She couldn't remember ever being so rattled by the mere presence of a man. She had to get control of herself.

"About twenty-five hundred acres," Rand told her. "We mostly raise beef cattle because the land's best suited for grazing. We grow a few crops. We're planting winter wheat now. We raise Thoroughbred horses, and there are a couple of gas wells on the property."

70

"You can see why we need a secretary who isn't afraid of diversity. Of necessity, every aspect of our business is different," Tara added.

"I hope she told you that she's a city girl and doesn't know a thing about ranching," Mike felt obliged to inject, grinning and tugging a lock of Maggie's hair.

"I remind you that you grew up in the house next door to mine," Maggie returned his taunt. "That technically makes you as much of a city slicker as me."

Her teasing brought laughter. Rand crossed his arms over his chest and added, "As I see it, I'm the only one of this bunch who's one hundred percent country. All the rest of you are city born and bred."

His words met with a lot of moaning and groaning. Maggie dared a glance at Curt and found his eyes locked on her.

"You were a city boy when you first came to the ranch?" She couldn't resist asking. He'd tried to convince her that a city girl would be out of place on the ranch.

"I was born in New York," he responded without expression. "That doesn't mean I ever had a taste for city life."

He was reiterating his declaration about not wanting involvement with her. Maggie got the message, but the others were just surprised to hear him discuss anything personal. Curt wasn't known for his communication skills, especially with women.

"I didn't know you were from New York!" Tara exclaimed, her eyes going to Curt.

"A lifetime ago." His words were clipped and dismissive. He gave Tara a brief smile, putting an end to the matter without offending her.

"You're originally from the city, too?" Maggie asked Tara.

"I was raised in Atlanta, Georgia," the other woman explained. "But I'm *never* leaving this ranch again!" The heartfelt intensity of her words generated more laughter.

"It's an inside joke," Mike told Maggie, wrapping his arm around her shoulders again. "Tara tried to shake the Oklahoma dust from her feet, but she couldn't get it out of her heart."

"I'll tell you about it sometime," Tara promised with a grin. Then she glanced at her watch. "Right now I'd better get to town and pick Mindi up from preschool."

"I'll go get her," Rand insisted. "You're going to take a nap before she gets home."

Tara started to argue, but her husband shook his head. "Nap time," he reiterated, his tone firm.

Tara sighed and rolled her eyes, then smiled at Maggie. "I think I'll take a nap. You can stay for supper, can't you? Then we can visit, and I'll be able to show you your rooms."

"I'd be happy to stay, if it won't mean a lot of extra work for you," Maggie responded.

"Heavens no, Geraldine cooks enough food for an army."

Rand explained. "Geraldine Jackson has been on the ranch longer than I have. She's in her eighties, but she still controls the kitchen and keeps us well fed. She'll love having another woman to coddle."

"Curt, you'll stay for supper, won't you?" Tara asked.

"Of course he will," Mike injected.

"I have work to do at home," Curt countered.

Maggie wondered if he normally ate with the family. She didn't like to think he was depriving himself just to avoid her.

"Oh, please stay," Tara coaxed lightly. "That way Maggie can get to know everyone before she starts working."

There had been a time when Tara and Curt were very wary of each other. During the past few months, they'd gained a mutual respect. Now, he rarely refused a request of hers.

"I guess I can make time for one of Geraldine's meals," he conceded with a slight grin.

Maggie thought it was indecent the way that little tilt of his lips made her heartbeat accelerate, even when it was being directed at someone else.

"That's settled then," Rand declared. "I'm going for Mindi, Tara's taking a nap, and we'll trust you two to show Maggie around. See that she finds her way to the dining room in time for supper."

"You got it, boss," Mike agreed, hugging Maggie close to his side. "I've got a lot of catching up to do with the midget, so I'll give her the grand tour."

Maggie noted a flare of anger in Curt's eyes as Mike hugged her again. He looked irritated by Mike's possessive attitude, and she couldn't imagine why he should care. He certainly hadn't wanted anything to do with her.

Belatedly, she realized that he hadn't heard her explain that Mike was her cousin. She wondered what Curt was thinking.

Rand and Tara left them, and they turned toward the barns, heading to where the two foremen had been loading rolls of wire fence on a pickup truck.

"I'll take the fencing to the crew while you show

Ms. Malone around,'' Curt volunteered, wanting to put some distance between himself and the lady in question.

"Damn!" Mike growled. "I forgot they're waiting for that fencing. I'll take it out; you're not even supposed to be working today.''

"No problem," Curt clipped.

"Hell, yes, it's a problem. This is supposed to be your day off and you've already spent half of it helping me. I'll take the fencing. Just be polite to Maggie until I get back.''

"Can't I go with you?" she asked, suddenly appalled at being thrust on Curt when he obviously didn't want to spend time with her.

"Not in that outfit, Midget," Mike argued as he swung his big body into the driver's seat of the pickup. "The truck's filthy, and it's a muddy mess in that pasture. I won't be long.''

The engine roared to life, and Maggie was swiftly abandoned by her cousin. She stood, hands on hips, glaring at the retreating truck.

"What is it about me that makes men think they can just brush me aside like an insect?" she demanded irritably, her eyes flashing to Curt's, her temper simmering. "And don't tell me that I'm no bigger than an insect,'' she snapped.

"Maybe men just want to be protective," Curt responded, starting to move toward the barn.

Maggie grabbed his arm and halted him, then quickly withdrew her hand when his eyes flashed in warning. The reminder of what had transpired between them earlier took some of the heat from her temper.

"I am an intelligent, responsible adult," she stated very clearly. "Why does everyone assume I need protecting?''

"Probably because you're petite and beautiful."

Curt's eyes were cool, and his compliment was made in such a matter-of-fact fashion that Maggie was temporarily taken aback.

Her crazy heart refused to regulate when his eyes rested on her. "You think I'm beautiful?" she couldn't help but ask.

"Did you ever doubt it?" he queried derisively.

Maggie turned her head from his piercing gaze. She wasn't sure how to respond. She was pleased with her appearance, but she hadn't always been. Sometimes the insecurities still nagged at her, but those feelings were hard to explain.

"I was always such a scrawny kid," she grumbled. "I used to be terribly self-conscious about my skinny body and wild hair. It's taken me a long time to adjust to the changes, and sometimes I still have trouble handling comments about my looks."

Curt knew she was serious, not just being coy. He couldn't see a thing to worry about, though. Anyone with half a brain could tell that her beauty was the kind that went deep and lasted a lifetime.

"You'd better get used to compliments," he told her, heading for the barn again. "This place is crawling with unattached males who'll go crazy when they get a look at you. You'll appreciate your sweetheart's protection then."

"Sweetheart?" Maggie echoed as she followed Curt into the darkness of a barn. She was assaulted by hot, heavy air and unfamiliar smells, as well as temporary blindness. She hesitated.

Curt took hold of her arm and guided her toward the center of the barn. An open window in the hayloft lit the interior with a shaft of sunlight. They were surrounded by rows of empty stalls. Maggie assumed the horses were all outside.

Curt's hold on her was light, and he broke the contact as quickly as possible. Still, warmth permeated her whole body, making her wonder if Curt's affect on her hormones was natural.

"Sweetheart?" she challenged again, refusing to let him ignore her question.

"Mike."

"Mike isn't my sweetheart."

"Lover?" he growled, his muscles tensing at the thought. His eyes speared her. "You didn't mention that you were coming to the McCain ranch because of a lover."

Maggie glared right back at him. He had the nerve! He'd made it clear that he wasn't interested, but he had the audacity to hassle her over her relationship with Mike. What an ego!

"Mike is my cousin."

Curt's grunt was disbelieving. "Kissing cousins? He couldn't keep his hands off you. Do all your cousins fondle you like a lover?"

Maggie's mouth and eyes went wide. "That's a disgusting thing to say!" she snapped, stepping closer to him in her anger.

They were within inches of one another, and their eyes locked in a heated battle. The tension between them increased, despite their individual decisions to avoid another confrontation. It was much the same as earlier in the day, but this time Maggie was infuriated by Curt's churlish attitude.

"Mike is my only cousin, and he's like a brother!" she declared hotly. "Our mothers are sisters, and we were practically raised together. We've always been close, and he can touch me whenever he wants!''

Curt reached out and touched her then. He took hold of both her arms and drew her close to his chest. He knew he was making a mistake. He knew she was telling the truth about her relationship with Mike, but the memory of the other man's arms around her made him feel murderous.

Maggie tried to pull away from him, but his hold on her tightened, drawing her closer until she could feel the hard length of him pressed against her. The contact was searing, making her voice go low and husky when next she spoke.

''You told me you didn't want anything to do with me,'' she reminded him hoarsely. ''Why should you care if Mike shows me a little affection?''

Curt's already taut features hardened more. His eyes blazed at the thought of other men touching her. He knew it was insane. He knew he was being a jerk. He knew he was asking for trouble in a big way.

None of the mental warnings seemed as important as staking a claim to an independent lady who had gotten under his skin in a major fashion. He drew her even closer, until he could smell the sweetness of her perfume and feel the delicate trembling of her body.

Their eyes locked again. The fire in Curt's nearly stole what was left of Maggie's breath. Her lungs constricted. She wanted to insist that he answer her question, but breathing was suddenly too difficult.

For a long time, Curt just held her tightly. Maggie's hands were trapped between their bodies, and she could feel the violent pounding of his heart. Her heart beat a matching rhythm.

She wanted his mouth on hers more than she'd ever

wanted anything in her entire life. Even the memory of his brutal kiss couldn't dampen the wanting. She needed to know what it felt like to really be kissed by him. And she wanted him to want it every bit as much as she did.

Her eyes darted to his mouth, her tongue involuntarily moistening her own dry lips, and then she dared look directly at Curt again. His eyes blazed with barely controlled hunger. Maggie knew it was daring and risky, but she wanted to smash his control.

"Go ahead," she taunted him huskily, lifting her lips as her eyes challenged him sassily. "Teach me another lesson."

Curt's eyes blazed into hers. His heart slammed against her chest, and she felt the pulsing strength of his arousal against her thighs. He made her feel wild, reckless, hungry.

She made him feverish with desire. He was harder and hungrier than he'd ever felt in his life. His control was disintegrating, his need was savage, and still she taunted him.

Maggie recognized his monumental battle for control. She knew that he didn't want to want her, and that he still might deprive her of his kiss. "Be brave," she urged huskily.

Curt's hard mouth took her sassy one with a fervor that stunned them. His lips locked with hers, and his tongue plunged between her teeth for a more intimate mating.

Maggie's head was forced backward, but this time she returned the pressure with a hunger of her own. She closed her eyes and moaned softly at finally getting a sweet taste of Curt's passion. She tilted her head to urge him closer and sucked his tongue deeper into her mouth.

His body bucked in reaction to her responsiveness. The moan that escaped his throat was low and long. His hands grasped her hips and pulled her into the cradle of his thighs. His blood pulsed hotly through his body. He wanted to crawl inside her and ease the throbbing ache she'd created.

Maggie managed to ease her hands from between their bodies and wrap them around Curt's neck. She hugged him more tightly and moaned softly when he crushed her closer.

His tongue continued to plunder her mouth. The kiss had grown less aggressive and more exploratory. They strained to learn the taste and textures of each other. Their lips parted briefly for air, then locked again with renewed fervor.

Maggie's fingers slid into the thickness of Curt's hair, touching him as she'd wanted to do last night and this morning. Her fingers clenched and unclenched in the soft, heavy waves, gently urging him closer as she thrust her tongue into his hot mouth.

Curt accepted her offering with a tortured groan. He sucked gently, then fiercely, then gently again on her honeyed sweetness. He didn't release her mouth until they were both starved for breath.

Maggie opened her eyes and looked directly into his. She wondered if hers looked as glazed as Curt's did. His shone with passionate need that seared her soul. She captured his mouth again, and he didn't resist the renewed mating of lips, teeth, and tongues.

He wanted to memorize the taste and feel of her. He knew this should stop, but he wasn't ready to release her. The gentle suction of her soft mouth around his tongue staggered his breathing, made his blood run hot and his whole body hard.

He loved the heat of her sweet breath in his mouth. He loved the tightness of her fingers clutching his hair. He loved the feel of her breasts crushed to his chest, their nipples hard with arousal. He wanted her closer.

Curt shifted, wedging one strong thigh between hers, and Maggie gasped. Her skirt rode up. Her hose and underwear offered little protection from the erotic feel of his muscled, jean-clad leg being thrust against the heart of her femininity. When his hands on her hips rocked her against the rigid evidence of his desire, Maggie's breath broke into strangled gasps.

She grasped fistfuls of his hair and tugged viciously, demanding that Curt allow her to catch her breath. Everything was happening too fast. She was losing control. It was wild and wonderful and utterly frightening.

"Curt?" she rasped hoarsely, breathing raggedly and searching his taut features for a clue of his feelings.

He was fully supporting her weight, and he didn't ease his fierce hold on her when he read the confusion in her eyes.

"Don't ask me for explanations," he managed gruffly. He eased a hand up her spine to lock in the softness of her hair. The other hand kept her firmly clasped against his thighs. "I warned you."

"You hate wanting me, don't you?" Maggie forced herself to ask. "Am I so unappealing? Is my body all that interests you?"

"It's definitely at the top of my list right now," he growled, recapturing her mouth.

This time his kiss was slow and gentle. His lips teased hers, his teeth nipped at the corners of her mouth, and then his tongue made a slow, sexy foray between her teeth again.

Maggie trembled in his arms. The kiss was nearly her undoing. She'd never experienced anything so addictive as Curt's kisses. She might have been able to resist another passionate onslaught, but she had little defense against such tenderness.

The tender feelings were foreign to Curt and alarming. He'd never wanted to kiss a woman breathless. He couldn't remember ever wanting to give so much time and attention to kissing a woman. Even though the rest of his body was on fire, he still wanted to investigate every inch of Maggie's mouth.

He wanted to explore every inch of her body, too. Her mouth was just an intriguing appetizer. He wanted to lavish attention on her breasts with his hands and then his mouth. He wanted to sheathe himself in her softness.

He wanted to spend days, maybe weeks, devouring her. But that was crazy. It couldn't happen. He'd never wanted or needed long-term involvement.

Slowly, in gradual stages, Curt ended the seduction of her mouth. Next he shifted his leg, gently forcing her to slide down his body onto her own feet. When she was standing perfectly still, he released her and stepped out of reach.

Maggie took a step, then two, backward, putting more distance between them. They eyed each other warily.

"This ends, here and now." Curt's features tensed as he issued the terse command.

Maggie lifted a hand and nervously smoothed her hair. She was badly shaken by her own loss of control and her unprecedented, uninhibited response to his embrace. Her body still trembled from aftershocks of the passionate exchange. She needed time to come to terms with her feelings for Curt.

"We hardly know each other," she argued while battling for her normal calm. "You said it's just physical. We can ignore it. We *will* ignore it!" She sounded hysterically emphatic.

"Right." Curt's mind was in agreement, even if his body was suffering a painful withdrawal.

"I want this job with the McCains, but I don't want to cause you any grief," Maggie continued, making decisions that she knew were right for both of them. "I know we can work together without letting chemistry take precedence over common sense."

"Right," Curt repeated. He ran a hand through his hair in agitation and took a deep breath. He knew she was right. So why did the carefully worded rejection add to his frustration?

Temporary madness. A moment of lustful insanity. Neither of them wanted it to happen again, thought Maggie as she straightened her clothing. She'd been curious about her strong attraction to Curt, but she hadn't been prepared for her violent reaction to his attentions. She didn't like the loss of control.

At the sound of a pickup returning to the barnyard, both of them frowned. Maggie's eyes silently questioned him on her appearance. She felt flushed, wrinkled, and uncharacteristically rattled after their embrace.

"You look fine," Curt told her, heading for the door.

Maggie followed slowly. She knew she didn't look fine, but hoped her disarray would be attributed to a trek through a hot barn.

Mike greeted them as soon as they stepped from the

barn into the sunlight. Maggie squinted at her cousin, hoping she didn't look as flushed as she felt.

"How's the tour going?"

"All we managed to see was the horse barn," said Curt.

Mike glanced from one of them to the other.

"Miss Malone has quite a curiosity." Curt offered a plausible excuse for their delay without lying to his friend.

Mike roared with laughter. Maggie felt her blush deepen at the double meaning in Curt's explanation. He'd warned her that her curiosity could lead to unexpected complications.

When Mike's laughter subsided, he pulled Maggie close to his side and hugged her. "This woman was born with the words what, when, where, how, and why on her lips. I've been answering her questions since she was old enough to speak."

"I can believe that," Curt replied, feeling less aggressive about the relationship between Mike and Maggie.

In response to Mike's teasing, she grabbed a handful of his whiskers and jerked hard. He howled, and she smiled.

"Damn, Midget, if you don't stop doing that, I'll have a naked face."

"I've seen your naked face," she reminded him unrepentantly. "It's not half as bad as that grisly beard."

Mike groaned, anticipating another lecture on why he'd grown his beard and why he intended to keep it.

Maggie didn't feel like lecturing, so she let him off the hook for now, but she intended to do a lot of lecturing during the coming months. The gleam in her eyes told him as much.

Mike groaned again and gave Curt a harried look. "Once this woman gets a bee in her bonnet, there's no peace in my life. She's been nagging me for years to go back to Chicago."

"You think Mike belongs in the city?" Curt queried, wondering if she had an ulterior motive for coming to the ranch.

"Probably not," replied Maggie. "But I know he has some unfinished business in Chicago."

Her words turned Mike's normally congenial countenance into a thundercloud. "Don't start, Midget," he warned.

Maggie gave Curt an impish grin that did crazy things to his insides. She continually amazed him. He'd never seen Mike looking so desperate, and the big man rarely lost his temper.

"I've already told Curt that I'm not here to cause anybody any grief. I just want to see if I'm suited for the ranch business. God knows I don't seem cut out for anything else worth having."

There was enough genuine frustration in her statement to defuse Mike's temper and activate his protective instincts. "You're going to be perfectly content here, Midget, I'm sure of it. I tried to coax you out here a few years ago."

"I know, but I wasn't ready a few years ago."

"Damned independent woman," Mike groused, giving her another bear hug. "Let's get on with this tour. I know you won't be satisfied until you've seen every inch of the place. You coming, Curt?"

"No." The other man didn't elaborate, just headed for his own pickup truck. "I'll see you later."

Mike and Maggie exchanged glances, then shared a

grin. "You have an amazing affect on men," he chided her. "I thought Curt was immune, but maybe not."

"Immune to what? Me as a person, as a sex object, or as potential co-worker and friend?"

"He's immune to women, period," Mike offered, directing Maggie to another of the three big barns on the property. "I've never seen any woman make an impression on him, but believe me, I've seen plenty try."

"He seems to like Tara," Maggie supplied, wondering if Curt's feelings for his employer's wife were more than casual.

"Tara managed to gain his respect. Curt keeps everybody at a respectful distance. He works harder than most and has the respect of everyone around here. I'd trust him with my life, but he doesn't encourage close friendships. I guess Rand is as close a friend as he's ever had."

"I wonder what makes him tick?"

"So do I," Mike admitted. "He's never been forthcoming with personal information, and I haven't pried."

"How can you stand it?" Maggie teased. When it came to curiosity, Mike's was every bit as intimidating as hers, but his was directed at understanding human emotions.

"I'm reformed," he told her.

"Like fudge, you are."

Mike barked out a laugh. "You know me too well."

"Does anyone else here know that you're a licensed psychiatrist?" she felt compelled to ask.

Mike shook his head, frowning. "Rand has my resumé on file, but it's not common knowledge. Since it has nothing to do with my work here, I don't want it generally known."

"Message received, loud and clear," she retorted, ducking inside another big barn.

"How about a promise?" Mike insisted, guiding her.

"What kind of promise?" she hedged, poking her nose into various areas of the building.

"A promise that you won't interfere in my personal life." His tone was adamant.

"Please, big guy, have a little faith. Have I ever invaded your privacy?" Maggie taunted.

"Let me count the ways," Mike insisted. "There was the time I wanted to give my first girlfriend a kiss and you kept peeking at us through the bushes."

"I couldn't have been more than four or five years old," Maggie argued. "You might be older, but you were still too young to be necking with girls in the backyard."

"The time you crashed a stag party I was hosting?"

"Those guys were delinquents. I was protecting you."

"And let's don't forget the time you took photographs of my skinny-dipping expedition at the Hendersons' pool."

Maggie giggled when reminded of that particular incident. She'd blackmailed Mike for months.

"Still think it's funny, huh?" he growled.

Maggie didn't respond, just giggled harder.

Mike gave her one of his fiercest scowls, but she broke into delighted laughter. He did, too. She'd been special to him since the day his Aunt Molly had brought her home from the hospital. He knew it was useless to try to intimidate her.

Maggie felt warmed by their familiar banter. She'd always depended on Mike to make her laugh and to make her feel at home wherever she might be.

"I can see you've become even more unmanageable in the last few years," Mike declared.

Maggie tossed her hair over her shoulder, lifted her chin, and stuck her nose in the air. The pose assured him that his remark didn't rate a verbal response.

Mike chuckled at her antics, then got on with the business of showing her the McCain property. Later, he would realize she hadn't given him a promise to keep quiet about his background.

SIX

Maggie spent most of October settling into the ranch routine. For the first few weeks, she barely left the office during the daytime and rarely left the ranch. She had a lot to learn and was impatient to know all the details of her new job.

Mike and a couple of ranch hands had gone with her to Dallas to collect her personal belongings. Rand loaned them a truck for hauling her furniture. The items she couldn't fit into her rooms at the ranch had been stored at Curt's house.

The problem of storage space had worried Maggie, and had become the topic of discussion on her first evening at the ranch. Rand, Mike, and Tara had come up with a temporary solution. Curt had agreed that he had plenty of space, and a decision was made. Maggie didn't mind storing her things at his ranch, but she'd avoided going there when her furniture was unloaded.

Her rooms at the ranch were more like an apartment. She had a huge bedroom, a bathroom complete with a small clothes washer and dryer, and a kitchenette.

The main part of the ranch house branched out with two sprawling wings on either side. The family and Geraldine had rooms in one wing, and the other wing was reserved for guests. Maggie's apartment was in this section, allowing her as much privacy as she wanted.

She joined the family for lunch and supper during the week, but usually fended for herself on the weekends. She liked Geraldine, Mindi, and all the ranch employees.

Geraldine was a dear, and insisted on mothering her. Mindi was a bright, energetic little girl, and they'd become firm friends. All the unattached males on the ranch, except for Curt, had asked her out and had been charmingly refused.

In her first month of work, Maggie made it clear that she was a dedicated professional. Her enthusiasm never flagged. She proved that she was efficient, reliable, and had a tendency to work too hard.

Despite her firm but tactful refusal to date, she managed to befriend everyone. She always had a smile and a kind word to share. In a short time, she endeared herself to the entire staff.

Curt didn't speak to her unless he had to. Maggie had been sure if they ignored the attraction between them, it would die a natural death, but it didn't. Her pulse still skipped into high gear when they were in the same room or when she heard the sound of his voice.

After a month, Maggie was content with the progress she'd made and with her new job. She'd learned a lot of the basics about the ranch business. The McCains were easy to work for, and their growing confidence in her was evident.

The weather remained mild, with an occasional thunderstorm. November began with a promise of more pleasant weather. On a sunny Saturday at the beginning of the month, Maggie spent the morning in the office, but decided to spend the afternoon outdoors, getting some fresh air and exercise.

She dressed in old jeans and a royal blue sweater. Then she fastened her hair at her nape with a large barrette, and headed out the back door. She hadn't gotten far when she found Mindi sitting on the porch steps, looking dejected.

"Hi, Mindi, whatchadoin'?" Maggie asked the little girl who was a miniature replica of her mother with dark, curly hair and bright hazel eyes.

"I'm bored," replied Mindi, sounding forlorn. Her chin was propped on her hands, her elbows on her knees. An expression of disgust masked her normally cheerful features.

Maggie smothered a grin. "That sounds serious. How could you be bored on such a lovely day?"

"I want to go swimmin', but Mama says no. Daddy says it's too cold, but it's not. I'm bakin' in this sun," she added for emphasis.

Maggie guessed that Mindi had just lost a disagreement with her parents. "There are plenty of other things to do on such a pretty day."

"Like what?"

"You could ride your pony."

"No fun by myself. Mama's taking a nap and Daddy's making sure she goes to sleep. I'm 'posed to behave."

There was so much disgust in the childish tones that Maggie couldn't help but be amused.

"Wouldn't you like to take a little nap, too?"

Mindi's eyes widened with horror, and Maggie

dropped the subject. "How about riding your bike? Or having a tea party with your doll babies?"

Mindi just kept shaking her head and looking bored.

"We could play hide and seek for a while."

"It's no fun with just two people," Mindi countered.

"We could fly a kite," Maggie suggested, warming to the idea when Mindi's eyes lit with interest.

Then the small face fell again. "I don't have a kite. I took mine to school, and I forgot to bring it home."

It had been years since Maggie flew a kite, but she'd always loved it. The breeze was strong enough, so she racked her brains for the necessary supplies.

"I think we can make our own kite," she told Mindi. "I made one once from a plastic bag. Then we just need some string, a couple of sticks, and something for the tail."

"I know where the bags are in the pantry, but I don't know about sticks and the other things," Mindi told her, showing more enthusiasm.

"I'm sure Mike or one of the other guys can find us some sticks. They probably have some string, too. The tail is easy. We can use an old sock, or I can cut up a pair of panty hose."

That made Mindi giggle. She bounced to her feet. "I'll get the bag and see if Geraldine has any string."

"You can get a pair of hose from my room, too," Maggie told her. Mindi was a frequent visitor to her rooms and knew where almost everything was located. "The hose are in the top left drawer of my dresser."

"Okay, I'll find some."

"And I'll find Mike," Maggie declared.

"Mike's not here," Mindi remembered with a frown. "He went to town with the other guys. Curt's the only one here."

Maggie wasn't pleased with the information, but she didn't want to disappoint Mindi. "I'm sure Curt can help us."

Mindi was shaking her head, making her curls bounce. The frown had returned to her face. "Curt probably won't help. He doesn't like me."

Mindi's declaration shocked Maggie. She could tell the child was serious. "What ever gave you that idea?"

Curt often joined the family for meals. He never displayed much emotion on any topic but ranching, so she knew he'd never done anything to make Mindi think he disliked her.

"He never talks to me or gives me a piggyback ride or even smiles at me. I think he doesn't like little girls."

"I'm sure you're wrong," Maggie insisted. "Maybe Curt just doesn't know what to say to little girls. Maybe he thinks you don't like him."

"I like him," Mindi injected.

"Have you ever told him you liked him or asked him to play with you?"

"No, 'cause he doesn't smile as much as Mike and my daddy."

"Well then, let's see if we can make him smile," Maggie suggested. "Maybe somebody needs to teach him how to play."

Mindi's eyes began to sparkle, and her head was bobbing in agreement. "My mama told my daddy that Curt works too hard. We can show him how to fly a kite. That's play."

"Good idea," Maggie assured her. "You go tell Geraldine we're making a kite, and tell her you'll be with me for a while. I'll go find Curt."

When Mindi was gone, Maggie took a deep breath

and headed for the barns. She was annoyed with herself for her continued fascination with Curt. He hadn't done or said anything in the past weeks to suggest he was interested in her.

He was polite, but his attitude was always impersonal. There'd been no repeat of the intimacy they'd shared a month ago. Still, her pulse fluttered, and she grew heady with anticipation at the thought of being near him.

Maybe it was his indifferent attitude, she mused as she crossed the barnyard. Maybe her interest stemmed from his disinterest. His cool detachment piqued her, so her fascination could be attributed to the challenge of breaking through his reserve. Maybe she'd find him less appealing if his manner weren't so distant.

Familiarity breeds contempt, Maggie reminded herself as she entered the barn. If she got to know him really well, perhaps she wouldn't be so intrigued by him. But how could she get to know him better when he was determined to ignore her?

"Curt!" she called to him from just inside the horse barn. Regardless of her decision to challenge him, she didn't want to do it where they'd shared their passionate embrace.

"Curt!" she called again. There was a faint reply, and Maggie stepped a little farther into the building.

"Coming!" Curt shouted at her.

Maggie heard him moving toward her and decided to back out of the barn. Not because she was a coward, but because it was easier to see outdoors.

"What's wrong?" Curt asked as he joined her.

Maggie's annoyance increased with her pulse rate. She carried a mental picture of Curt with her always, yet the sight of him still caught at her breath. Dressed as usual in faded jeans and a faded cotton shirt, he was gorgeous.

"Nothing's wrong," Maggie assured. "I just need a little help, and Mindi said everyone else has gone to town."

"What kind of help?" Curt asked without expression. He had grown accustomed to controlling his physical reaction to Maggie in the past month. He knew it was for the best, and she'd made it easier by following his lead.

"Mindi and I have decided to make a kite, but we need help."

Curt's brows rose in amazement, and his tone expressed his skepticism. "You want me to help make a kite?"

Maggie wasn't pleased by his reaction. "You seem to be able to make anything else you want," she reminded him.

It was the first time she'd alluded to the night they'd shared at his house, and she knew it caught him off guard. His eyes narrowed.

"I know how to put the thing together," she continued defensively. "But I need a couple of sturdy, flexible sticks to use for the frame."

Her words sounded short and clipped, but Curt was looking at her as though she'd committed some sort of unpardonable act.

"I'll see what I can find," he replied.

He started to turn away, and Maggie cursed her own cowardice. Taking a deep breath, she halted him with her next words.

"Mindi and I would also like to have you help us fly the kite."

Curt turned slowly and looked directly into her eyes, with one brow cocked in a questioning fashion.

"Mindi thinks you don't like her."

It was plain to see that her declaration surprised him.

"Where did she get that idea? I don't remember ever saying a harsh word to her."

"You don't say *anything* to her and you never offer her piggyback rides. She assumes it's because you don't like little girls," Maggie charged softly. Her dark eyes challenged him on a very personal level for the first time in a month. "She says you don't smile enough and you don't play at all."

Curt cursed his gut reaction to the daring gleam in Maggie's eyes. He hated to admit it, but he'd missed her provocative banter. He'd thought his desire for her had lessened until she attacked him with her sassy eyes and mouth.

"Women!" he muttered, shaking his head in resignation. "How long should the sticks be?" He ignored the taunt about not playing enough.

Maggie grinned, her heart rejoicing at his small concession. "About a yard each, I think."

"Doesn't one have to be shorter?"

"Just a little if we make the traditional shape."

Curt headed for a large toolshed where all types of lumber were stored. Maggie followed, warning herself to tread softly. She was thrilled at the thought of spending time with Curt, but she didn't want to push her luck.

Mindi came running across the barnyard with a plastic bag, a spool of string, and a pair of nylon stockings. Maggie smiled and called for her to join them. Mindi ran to the shed, her face beaming with pride.

"I got everything!" she exclaimed.

"You did a great job," Maggie praised, accepting all the supplies Mindi had gathered. "Did you remember to tell Geraldine that you'd be busy with me for a while."

"Yep. She says she thinks she'll just take a nap, too, since I'll be with you."

"Geraldine didn't want to help fly the kite?" Curt asked, giving Mindi his full attention.

She giggled, glanced at Maggie, and giggled harder.

Maggie was grinning, too. The image of Geraldine flying a kite was highly amusing. The elderly lady wasn't any taller than Maggie, but she was almost as round as she was tall.

"I think Curt is teasing us," Maggie told Mindi.

The little girl's eyes widened and flew to Curt's. "Were you just teasing us?"

Curt gave her the half smile that made Maggie's breath scatter. "Maybe just a little," he admitted.

Mindi grinned and nodded in satisfaction. "That's okay. My mama says everybody in this family is a terrible teaser."

Maggie laughed and Curt shook his head. Then they got busy with their kite construction. Curt picked out the wood while Maggie and Mindi folded the bag in the proper shape.

A staple gun was used to attach the bag to the sticks. Curt tied the string to the kite while Maggie ripped enough nylon from her hose to make a tail. Then they found a smooth round stick to hold the ball of string.

"That should do it," Maggie announced when they'd completed their handiwork. She held up the kite and handed the string to Mindi. "It's just perfect. Now where shall we fly it?"

"Not too close to electric lines," Mindi repeated the lesson she'd been given at preschool.

"And not too close to the barns or house," Maggie added. "How about the pasture behind the horse barn?"

Mindi and Curt both shook their heads. "Cow pies," they declared in unison. When Curt winked at the little girl, she giggled happily.

The wink warmed Maggie's heart, even if it wasn't directed at her. "So where do we go?"

"How about the front yard?" suggested Curt. "There's plenty of room out there and nothing in the way."

"Yes! Yes!" Mindi squealed in delight, skipping out of the shed. "That's where we should go!"

Curt and Maggie followed her, but Curt hesitated when they continued across the barnyard.

"You're coming with us, aren't you?" Maggie halted long enough to ask the question and Mindi was forced to stop, too.

"Please, Curt!" Mindi begged, holding her free hand out to the big man. "It's goin' to be lots of fun!"

Curt's eyes flew to Maggie's. Finding little support, he looked back at Mindi. "What if I don't know how to fly a kite?"

"We'll teach you! We'll teach you!" she chanted, skipping to his side and grabbing one of his hands.

Curt gave her hand an unexpected tug, pulling her closer, then he grasped her around the waist and swung her onto his shoulders. Mindi squealed with delight, and clung to both the kite string and his head.

"Look at me, Maggie. I'm taller than anybody!"

"You certainly are," Maggie agreed, smiling up at Mindi and then dropping her eyes to Curt's. His were warmer than she'd ever seen them, except in passion.

Her heart did a crazy little somersault. "I feel like a midget."

Mindi giggled. "That's what Mike always calls you."

"If you're a good little girl," Curt told Maggie softly, "maybe I'll let you take a ride."

Maggie's eyes widened and her mouth opened, but she couldn't immediately formulate a reply to his outrageous suggestion. She could hardly believe he'd issued such a personal challenge. A mental image of herself on his shoulders was blatantly provocative, as she was sure he knew.

"Just keep your mind on kite flying," she finally managed a softly spoken retort. "I'm not interested in a ride."

Maggie thought she heard a disgusted snort, but Mindi's excited chatter interrupted their private exchange.

"Can you get the kite in the air?" she asked as they reached the open yard in front of the house. "You have to run fast."

"Give me a lot of extra string," Maggie instructed, moving away from the twosome. "I'll try to get it up, and then you'll have to control it with the string on your stick."

She ran across the yard, holding the kite aloft until the wind caught it and lifted it from her hands. On the first couple of tries, the kite swiftly nose-dived to the ground, but before long, they had it airborne. Maggie instructed Mindi to let the string out gradually, so that the kite didn't fly too far.

They all watched as the kite soared higher. Mindi cheered, bouncing up and down on Curt's shoulders. The next time the kite did a dive, he swung her to the ground so that she could run and keep it aloft.

Maggie cheered her efforts and laughed happily when Mindi ran faster. She ran back and forth across the yard until she was panting from exertion. Every time the kite dove dangerously close to a treetop, Curt snatched Mindi into the air, and they managed to avert disaster.

When Mindi's arms grew tired, she gave Maggie a turn at flying the kite and flopped to the ground. Maggie reeled some of the string in and explained her favorite way to handle the kite.

"I like to keep it close, where I can see it," she told them, sitting down beside Mindi on the thick grass. "Then I like to lie on my back, and watch the kite dance on the clouds."

Mindi giggled again and began describing the clouds. Maggie stretched out on her back and rested the ball of string on her stomach. Her eyes beckoned to Curt.

He hesitated briefly, but joined them on the ground. Mindi was on Maggie's left side, so he dropped down on her right. He stretched out on his back, propped his head on his hands, and followed the kite with his eyes.

The ground was warm beneath them. The grass cushioned their bodies comfortably. The sun bathed them in more warmth, and everyone lazily watched as the kite waltzed with fluffy clouds on a field of blue.

Mindi's chatter gradually quieted to mumbles, and then her eyelids grew heavy and drooped. Maggie smiled when the child finally lost her battle with exhaustion and fell asleep.

"I think our little kite flyer wore herself out," she told Curt a short time later, breaking the companionable silence.

Curt turned on his side, propping his head on one hand while the other reached toward the string resting on Maggie's stomach. He plucked the taut line and felt the pull of the kite.

"I've never flown a kite before," he told her.

Maggie's eyes widened and locked with his. "Never?" she asked in amazement. "Not even when you were little?"

"Never," Curt returned. "Where I lived, there wasn't room for anything, especially not flying a kite."

"But you said you grew up in New York," Maggie insisted softly. "There are parks and school yards."

Overcrowded, dangerous parks and cluttered school yards. Curt wasn't sure how to explain without sounding like he wanted sympathy. He remembered the slums he'd lived in by the lack of space, lack of fresh air, and lack of privacy.

"I guess I just never made time," he said, taking the stick holding the string from her hands. He lay flat again and took control of the kite.

Maggie turned on her side and faced him, her eyes studying him closely as he enjoyed the simple pleasure of flying the kite. She wondered what his childhood must have been like. He obviously didn't want to discuss it, but she knew his memories were far removed from her remembrances of a carefree childhood.

"When did you move from the city?"

"When I was old enough to join the army."

"Eighteen?" Maggie queried as her eyes continued to study the strong lines of his face. She was sorely tempted to reach out and touch him, but she resisted the urge.

"I lied about my age and joined when I was sixteen."

Maggie's eyes widened farther. "How could you?

What about school? Didn't you need your parents' signatures or something?''

"My parents died before I started school. I was raised by relatives and earned my high school diploma in the service.''

Maggie was frustrated by the bare facts and no details, but her active imagination was filling in the blanks. He must have felt bereft growing up without his parents. She imagined Curt's childhood had been a very lonely one, lacking in love and emotional security.

"Why did you choose to join the army?'' she asked him.

"It was a cheap escape route.'' His tone lacked emotion, but when his eyes met Maggie's, they dared her to doubt him.

"Did you find the escape you wanted?''

"Yes,'' Curt responded, shifting his eyes back to the sky. "The army gave me a look at the world outside the city, and I earned enough money to buy my own land.''

"That was important?''

"That was most important.''

"Have you always wanted to be a rancher, or did you decide to locate in Oklahoma after you met Rand?''

Curt was quiet for a moment while he tried to formulate a response to questions he'd never answered before. He couldn't find the words to describe the yearnings of a poor boy with big dreams of wide, open space and abundant fresh air.

"I knew I wanted to settle in the west. When I met Rand, he suggested I try Oklahoma. He even had land that I could buy.''

Maggie gave in to the urge to touch him. She brushed

her fingers lightly over his knuckles, and was pleased to feel his grip on the stick relax.

"You're very lucky, you know."

Curt's eyes locked with hers. "I don't think I ever considered myself lucky."

"You're lucky to know what you want in life, where you belong, and that you're perfectly suited to the life you've chosen."

He considered her words. "Haven't you always known who you were and what you wanted?"

Maggie's brows creased in a frown. "I've always had an abundance of self-confidence and emotional support. I'm comfortable with who I am, but I can't seem to find anyplace to belong."

As soon as the words were out of her mouth, she regretted them. She didn't want to sound pathetic. "I didn't mean to imply that I'm not a happy person. I know I'm one of the truly fortunate people of this world. It's just hard to explain my desire to be needed and to belong."

"I understand," Curt told her.

Maggie believed he really did understand. She sighed softly, sat up, and wrapped her arms around her knees. "I really love it here. I haven't had such good feelings about any other place I've ever lived and worked."

"Rand and Tara think you're a godsend," Curt said, reaching up to unclasp the barrette at her nape. He tossed it aside and ran his fingers through the silky strands of her hair.

Maggie sighed with pleasure and tipped her head backward to give him better access. Her scalp tingled from the gentle pull on her heavy tresses. Curt slowly drew her down beside him until he could cradle her head on his shoulder.

"Your hair is beautiful."

"Thank you," Maggie replied softly. Their mood was languorous and her heart was drumming a slow, heavy cadence.

She barely dared to breathe. She didn't want to do or say anything that might destroy the growing rapport between them. She knew Curt shared little of himself with anyone and she was thrilled that he felt he could trust her.

"I didn't mean to scare you that day in the barn."

Curt's words sent a ripple of erotic sensations over Maggie's body. The memory of the kisses they'd shared still had the power to excite her. The memory also made her wary, but she didn't want Curt to think he'd offended her in any way.

"*You* didn't scare me," she emphasized softly. "*We* scared me." The intensity of what they had shared was beyond her experience. She'd needed time to come to terms with a desire so strong that it shattered her control and common sense.

Curt had thought that his unbridled passion destroyed the tentative trust she'd given to him. He knew it shouldn't matter, but it did.

"I guess we're a pretty explosive pair," he declared in a low tone.

"Just chemistry?" Maggie queried lightly, though her heart was racing.

"Yeah," was Curt's flat rejoinder.

"I suppose we should continue to ignore it."

"Yeah."

SEVEN

It was a Friday almost two weeks later when Rand entered the ranch office in the late afternoon, seeking Maggie's assistance.

"Can you take a Jeep to the north pasture and find Curt? He went out on horseback to check some fencerows. He had a portable phone and was supposed to call me if he needed a crew sent out there. He hasn't called, and I don't want to leave the ranch until Mike's crew gets back."

"I don't mind," Maggie responded, rising from her seat at the computer and stretching her stiff muscles. "I need a chance to get some kinks out of my system."

"You spend too much time at that damned computer," Rand repeated his regular lecture. He was always telling Maggie she needed to get outside more often. "You and Tara don't have any sense at all when it comes to that equipment."

Maggie just laughed. She lost all track of time when she was working, but she appreciated a break now and then.

"Tara's giving Mindi a bath, but she said she'll listen for the phone," Rand said as he followed Maggie out of the house.

"Isn't it a little early for Mindi's bath?"

"The little monkey decided to make mud pies with the water from a drinking trough. She's grimy and smells rotten."

Maggie laughed and climbed into a Jeep while Rand held the door for her. He reminded her to fasten her seat belt and slammed the door.

"Curt was headed north, along the fence that starts beyond the horse barn. Follow the dirt lane until you reach the first gate, then stay close to the fence line. I don't know what could be taking him so long. Maybe his phone isn't working. I can't get any response when I call him."

The Jeep's engine roared to life at the first turn of the switch. All the ranch vehicles were kept in good working condition, and all of them were equipped with car phones or CB radios.

"I'll call as soon as I find him," Maggie promised.

"Be careful. The ground is soft in a few spots."

"Okay," she agreed, turning the Jeep in the direction of the lane that ran between barns. Rand went ahead of her and opened the first gate, then waved as she drove from the barnyard across the pasture.

The ride was bumpy, but Maggie didn't mind. As Rand's faith in her increased, he began to trust her with more of the ranch errands. She liked the constant change of pace and was pleased to be learning something new every day.

When Maggie reached the second gate, she put the Jeep in park, opened the gate, drove through, and then climbed back out to close the gate behind her. She knew from stock reports that these pastures were filled with a small fortune in livestock. She didn't want to take a chance that they might escape their protective fencing.

The ride became bumpier, and Maggie was forced to drive at a very low speed to negotiate the rough ground. As she followed the fence line, she kept an eye out for any sign of Curt or his horse. She was almost five miles from the house when she sighted the big buckskin gelding that Curt rode.

Maggie stopped the Jeep a few yards from the horse, then quickly climbed from the vehicle. Her eyes were still searching for Curt, but she couldn't see him anywhere. For the first time since Rand had sent her out, she felt a touch of alarm.

"Curt!" she called, moving closer to his horse. "Curt!" she repeated, louder. She noted that the horse's reins had been looped over the top rung of the fence. That meant Curt had dismounted. He hadn't been thrown, and the horse didn't make any attempt to leave the spot beneath a tree where he'd been tied.

Maggie couldn't see Curt, and there was only one tree to block her vision of the entire area. She moved closer to the tree, tilted her head back, and looked through the branches. She felt stupid, but had no idea where else Curt could be.

He wasn't in the tree, and he wasn't anywhere else in sight. Maggie reached for the phone in the backpack on the horse and called Rand.

"I've found Curt's horse, but he's not here."

"Did you yell for him?"

"I called his name several times, but there's nothing out here except the cattle, his horse, and me."

"Mike's on his way back to the ranch. As soon as

he gets here, we'll come out and look around. Do you mind staying out there a while longer?"

"No," Maggie injected quickly. "I'll keep calling for Curt. Maybe he walked a long way down the fence."

She replaced the phone and stroked Curt's horse, talking gently to the animal as her eyes scoured the surrounding area. "Where did he go?" she asked aloud.

The horse snorted and pawed the ground. Maggie looked down and kicked a pile of newly fallen leaves. In all the old westerns she'd watched, people could always track someone by looking for signs on the ground. She didn't have the faintest idea how that was accomplished.

She bent down to study the patterns of the leaves, but couldn't see the imprint of boots. So much for her tracking abilities, she thought as she slowly moved around the trunk of the big tree.

A cry of alarm escaped her when she noticed a gaping hole in the ground several yards along the fence on the opposite side of the tree. "Curt!" she screamed, running toward the hole.

She fell to her knees beside the hole and strained to see into the darkness. "Curt! Are you down there? Curt!" she continued to yell. "Can you hear me? Are you all right? Curt!" she screamed at the top of her lungs.

There was nothing but darkness and silence in the hole. It was a narrow opening in the ground, barely wide enough to swallow a man the size of Curt, but Maggie knew he had stepped into the hole. She knew he was down there, but she didn't know how far down or if he was badly hurt.

"Curt!" she kept yelling. "Curt, please answer me," she begged, feeling sick with anxiety. If he was trapped and injured, how in the world could they get him out of there?

Maggie ran to the Jeep, opened the glove compartment, and located a flashlight. Then she ran back to the hole and fell to the ground on her stomach. She turned on the light and aimed the beam down the hole, but could see nothing.

"Curt!" Her screams grew more shrill. "Curt!"

Silence. Just darkness and silence. A sob caught in Maggie's throat, but she forced it down again. She had to stay calm and think of some way to help him.

The sound of an approaching vehicle had Maggie jumping to her feet and running to meet Rand and Mike. She launched herself at Mike the minute he stepped from the truck.

"Curt's fallen into a hole. I found it right after I talked to Rand. I've called and called, but he's not answering me," she said, hurrying them to the spot where Curt had fallen.

"Damn!" Rand snapped when he saw the gaping hole in the ground. "I thought we found all these damned holes."

"What do you mean?" asked Maggie. "What kind of holes are they?"

Rand dropped to the ground and called to Curt.

Mike explained. "Rand's grandfather let a gas company drill for natural gas in this pasture. They didn't find any, but their drills were wider than most and they didn't leave diagrams of where they drilled. They just covered the openings with slats of wood and some sod."

All three of them had dropped to their knees around

the hole. Rand continued to call for Curt and try to see into the darkness with the flashlight.

"Do you think time and weather eroded the protective covering?" Maggie asked.

"Probably," Rand replied grimly. "We just found out about the abandoned shafts a few years ago. We tried to find the holes and fill them with concrete to avoid an accident like this."

Rand went back to the phone on Curt's horse and called the ranch. He instructed his staff to bring out a tank of oxygen and to call his neighbor, Craig Sanderson, in case they needed his helicopter for an emergency airlift.

"This hole is really close to the fence. That's probably why we missed it," Mike surmised as he carefully removed splinters of wood and leaves from the opening.

"We have to get him out of there," Maggie insisted, her eyes locking with Mike's. "He might be badly hurt."

"We'll get him out," Mike promised, "but it might take a little while."

"No!" Maggie cried. "We have to get him out now. It will be dark in a couple of hours. He must be hurt or he'd answer us. We have to do something right now!"

Mike didn't like the frantic tone of her voice. He tried to reason with her. "We'll have to move slowly and carefully. These holes aren't lined with anything solid, so we can't risk dislodging the soil and sending it down on top of Curt."

Maggie paled and terror widened her eyes. Curt could be buried alive if they weren't careful. "Can't we lower something down there to pull him out?"

"We could if he was conscious and could hold on to it," Rand explained. "If we knew exactly what position he's in, we could try to lock something around him and pull, but without his help, we can't risk it.''

"Do you think he's hurt his head?"

She didn't like the concerned glances the men exchanged.

"What are you thinking?" she demanded. "Don't keep secrets from me!" She grasped Mike's arm and beseeched him to be completely honest with her.

"Why don't you head back to the ranch and tell Tara what's happening out here?" Rand suggested.

"No!" Maggie was adamant. "I'm not going anywhere and I want to know what you think has happened to Curt. Why isn't he answering us? Are these holes really deep?" she asked with a resurgence of panic.

"No," Mike assured her. "That's one thing in Curt's favor. None of the holes was more than twenty feet deep. The drill kept running into solid rock."

"Then Curt's fall would have been halted at the rock?"

"Probably," Mike told her.

"Then why the hell can't he answer us?" Maggie demanded. "The only way he could have gone down that hole was standing straight up, with his arms above his head. That should have protected him from a head injury. So why isn't he conscious?"

Rand and Mike exchanged another glance, then Mike offered a possible explanation. "There is a lot of natural gas in the ground around here."

Maggie's stomach rolled. She bit her lips to keep a cry of fear from escaping. Her eyes shifted frantically from Mike to Rand and back to Mike.

"I want you to tie a rope around me and let me go down there to check on him."

Her demand was met by shock and disapproval.

"No!" Rand clipped.

"No!" echoed Mike.

"It's too damned dangerous, Midget," Mike insisted, putting an arm about her shoulders.

"I won't be in any danger if you have some kind of belt around me to pull me back out," she argued, finding a measure of consolation with the unfolding of a plan. "You can ease me down and I can wrap a rope around Curt. Then you can pull both of us out of the hole."

The men didn't tell her the idea was insane, but they both shook their heads negatively.

"The walls of the hole might crumble if you bump them the wrong way," Rand explained. He couldn't let her take that kind of risk, but he admired her courage and determination.

"It's too unstable," Mike reiterated.

"Couldn't I reinforce the walls with something as I go down?" Maggie was desperate for a solution.

"I don't see how," Mike argued. "Anything we could use for temporary support would block your escape."

Maggie groaned. She hadn't thought of that, but she wasn't willing to concede defeat.

"I could try to pack the dirt tighter against the walls as I went. Then I'd know if any of the soil was really loose."

Mike continued to shake his head. "Forget it, Midget, we don't have any idea what the concentration of gas is down there. It could be instantly fatal. The water level might be just as dangerous and lethal." His words were harshly spoken. He knew he had to be brutally honest to prevent false hopes.

Maggie had to cover her mouth with her hand to

prevent a cry of fear from escaping. She wrapped an arm about her waist in a protective fashion as tremors shook her body. There were too many threats to Curt's life.

"He's not dead," she rasped, glaring at both men and daring them to argue with her. "I know he's not dead." She wasn't sure how she knew, but she knew. "We have to get him out of there!"

Another ranch vehicle pulled to a stop near them. A couple of the ranch hands jumped from the truck and brought an oxygen tank to Rand. He immediately started lowering an extension hose down the hole.

"You're pumping oxygen to Curt?" Maggie queried.

"Yes." Mike continued to answer her questions as he and Rand slowly lowered the oxygen hose. "Curt could just be suffering from a temporary blackout. The oxygen might revive him."

"Enough to make him fully conscious and able to help himself if we drop a rope?" Maggie wanted to know.

"It's possible," Rand said, but his tone wasn't optimistic. "If Curt's been short of oxygen for very long, he might be weak."

"Too weak to hang on to a rope," Maggie added, "but couldn't he knot it around his chest or something?"

"Not if his hands are over his head and he doesn't have any room to move," Mike pointed out the probable situation.

"If the shaft is that narrow, then he can't use his feet to climb, either, can he?" Maggie continued in frustration. "Even if he's not badly hurt, he'd be totally trapped."

The men's faces were grim. Pete Davis and Ron Sheperd, the two ranch hands who'd joined them didn't offer much hope. Both of them had worked with Curt for several years, and despite the strength they knew he possessed, their expressions didn't reflect any hope.

Maggie wasn't having it. She knew they would work like demons to rescue Curt, but they didn't have the physical capabilities to help. Pete was as big a man as Mike. Ron was smaller through the shoulders, but had a big belly. Neither would fit down the hole.

Rand's build was the closest to Curt's, but forcing someone else his size down the hole would put added pressure on the unstable ground around the shaft.

"I think I've reached him," Mike told them as he gently maneuvered the oxygen hose. He drew it up to measure and check for water, then lowered it back down the hole.

"The bottom is about eighteen feet down and has four or five inches of water, but Curt's boots will protect him from that. Stretched out, Curt is probably six feet. That leaves ten or twelve feet between him and the top of the hole."

The words ten or twelve feet kept spinning around in Maggie's mind. Curt was ten or twelve feet underground. Why did those particular numbers nag at her memory?

Rand continued to call to Curt, hoping that once he'd been supplied with oxygen, he'd be able to respond.

Maggie leaned close to the hole and strained to hear even the weakest sound. She could hear the gentle hiss of the oxygen. The only other sound she heard was the nagging repetition of the numbers ten and twelve, ten and twelve, ten and twelve, echoing in her mind.

"I know what we can do," she finally said when her brain came up with the solution she was seeking. Her tone was so calm and sure that she immediately had everyone's attention.

"Those field tiles you ordered were delivered last week," Maggie reminded Rand. "They're twelve feet long and have a diameter wide enough for me to crawl through. I know because Mindi and I checked them out. I think they're even wide enough to accommodate Curt's shoulders."

Mike and Rand looked at each other, their expressions registering growing comprehension and a touch of optimism.

Maggie hurriedly explained her plan. "We could ease a tile down the hole to fortify the walls. Then you can lower me down to Curt and I can secure some kind of rope or strap around him. You could pull us both up without any risk."

She didn't give them a chance to raise objections, just continued to outline her plan as the details came together in her mind. "There's oxygen down there now and the water's not high. If we can line the shaft with a concrete tile, it will offer all the protection Curt and I need."

All four men were looking at her with something close to awe in their eyes. She continually amazed them.

"It just might work, boss." Pete put in a good word for Maggie's plan.

"Sounds foolproof," added Ron. "Want me to get the backhoe and haul a tile out here, just to see if it'll fit?"

"You're sure you want to do this?" Rand asked Maggie. "It's not going to be easy, and we don't know what shape Curt might be in," he warned.

"He's alive. I know he is," she insisted. "I want to

go down there and get him. If the tile will fit in the hole, then I'll find a way to pull Curt through it, even if I have to break both his arms." Her attempt at humor brought smiles and a lot of head shaking.

"Damn, but I believe you would," said Rand. "What do you think, Mike?"

Mike studied his cousin's anxious expression. "If anyone can do it, the midget can. Why don't you have Craig bring the tile out with the 'copter? He can swing it close and we can position it upright to fit the hole. That way we don't have to disturb the ground with heavy equipment."

"Good idea," said Rand. "I'll call Craig. Pete, you and Ron head back to the barn. Bring us some heavy rope and leather harnesses. We'll have to rig some kind of safety belt for Maggie. Tell Tara what's happening, but make sure she doesn't come out here."

"Who's Craig?" Maggie asked Mike when they were alone for a minute.

"Craig Sanderson. His ranch neighbors some of Rand's land. He's a pilot and has his own small airport. He also has a helicopter."

"Thank God!" Maggie murmured huskily, dropping to the ground again. She and Mike carefully cleaned the area around the opening of the hole to prepare it for the tile.

"Curt!" she yelled into the hole, then strained to hear a response.

"It's damned quiet down there," Mike reminded her softly. "It's pitch-black, cold, and it's going to be a tight fit, even for you."

Maggie knew what he meant. Her claustrophobic fears were common knowledge in their family. Once Mike had playfully locked her in a closet, and she'd actually passed out from fear. Another time she'd hyperventilated when they'd tried to explore a crawl space under her parents' front porch.

"This is different, big guy. I'm not a baby anymore, and I'm not going to freak out on you. I'm going to help Curt."

Mike nodded his approval, but his eyes were worried. The oxygen might have been too late, and he didn't know how he could protect Maggie from what she might find at the bottom of the hole. He wasn't sure how she'd react if she couldn't revive Curt. All he could do was wait and see, and offer support.

Minutes seemed like hours as they waited for help, but less than half an hour passed before they heard the return of the ranch vehicle and the sound of an approaching helicopter.

The helicopter inched closer, a tile swinging from a towing chain. Ron and Pete hurried to the hole to help Mike and Rand steady the tile and guide it to the opening in the ground. There was a collective sigh of relief when it fit the opening and could be gently forced down the hole.

"I wish Craig could hover until we have Maggie and Curt out of this thing," said Rand.

"We're too close to the tree," put in Mike.

"Yeah," he agreed as the tile continued to slide down the shaft of the hole. They had lowered it as much as they felt safe when there was only a foot still above ground. "Call Craig and tell him to release the chain. We'll secure it around the tree trunk. Everybody stand clear."

Mike radioed a message to the pilot, then everyone stood behind the ranch vehicles when Craig let the heavy chain drop to the ground. Ron and Pete hurriedly secured it around the tree.

Rand pulled a denim jacket from his truck and handed it to Maggie. "You'll need all the protection you can get from those leather straps. Better put a jacket over your blouse."

Maggie was only wearing lightweight slacks and a cotton blouse, but she didn't want the extra padding.

"I don't want anything restricting my movements," she told him. "I'll be fine."

"Maggie!" Mike barked at her in annoyance. He only called her Maggie when he was upset with her.

"Your hide will be ripped to shreds," Rand grumbled. "We'll be pulling both you and Curt's dead weight up by those straps."

"He's not dead!" she nearly screamed at him.

"He's not conscious either," Mike reminded grimly. "He weighs two hundred pounds and you'll be bearing the brunt of his weight as well as yours."

"If his arms are over his head, I can fasten a strap around his chest. Then he'll be taking most of the pressure."

The men just shook their heads and gave her sympathetic looks. Their pessimism was beginning to annoy her immensely.

"Curt is not dead!" she declared angrily, turning so that Mike could fasten a leather harness around her midsection.

"If he's not dead, then *we* will be when he regains consciousness," Rand supplied roughly. "He's going to kill us for letting you risk your life."

"I am not risking my life!" Maggie insisted through clenched teeth. "This is a good, safe plan," she reiterated, already feeling heavily weighted by the harness they were strapping around her.

"The chain is secure around the lip of the tile and around a sturdy tree. It's not going to budge an inch. I couldn't snap this leather and rope with a thousand pounds of pressure. I am not at risk here, Curt is."

"Okay, Midget, it's your show," said Mike. "Just don't take any chances. If the gas is noxious, get the hell out of there. Kick the tile once if you want us to lower you farther. Kick it twice if you want us to bring you back up."

"Kick like hell if anything scares you. If you haven't reached Curt by the time you get to the bottom of the tile, then let us bring you up and get a longer length of tile. Okay?" Rand wanted her promise to be cautious.

Maggie nodded. She couldn't force words past the lump in her throat. Now that she had to face the reality of the dark, narrow tile, her imagination was running wild. All the old phobias surfaced, but she determinedly battled them. She didn't have time to be afraid. Curt's life might depend on her courage.

"Here's a vial of smelling salts. When you get close to Curt, snap it with your fingers and hold it as close to his nose as you can," Rand instructed.

Mike was fitting a portable miner's light on her head. "This will help dispel some of the darkness."

Next Rand handed her a leather lead strap. "Slip this around Curt's shoulders. Clip the latch to the metal ring on your harness. Then hang on to him and try to let his body take most of the strain."

Maggie started to object, but Mike silenced her. "Curt's as strong as a horse and just as hard. You won't be putting him in any danger."

"Okay, let's do it," said Maggie.

Rand and Mike lifted her as though she weighed nothing. Maggie went into the tile headfirst with her arms stretched out in front of her. "Keep talking to me, Mike," she commanded gently as she took a deep breath.

"You got it, Midget," he agreed as he and Rand relinquished hold of her body and let her slide deeper into the tile. They kept a firm grip on her support system so that she wouldn't drop too quickly.

"We pulled the oxygen hose out of the tile so that you wouldn't get tangled. The hole should be full of pure air by now. If breathing gets difficult, kick three times and we'll send you more oxygen," Mike instructed.

He continued a monologue of instructions that were a repeat of everything she'd already been told. Maggie was reminded that she loved him dearly. He was always her champion even when he wasn't pleased with what she was doing. Having him close and hearing his voice was reassuring as darkness enveloped her.

It felt like all the blood in her body rushed to her head. As soon as she was being suspended completely by her harness, she felt the pull of gravity battling the restraints on her chest. The light on her forehead afforded some relief from total darkness, but there wasn't room to lift her head very high, so she couldn't really see too far ahead of her.

Mike and Rand continued to orchestrate her descent. Maggie was glad she didn't have to force herself to go deeper. Every muscle in her body was in shock.

The blood was pounding a pagan rhythm in her head. She forced herself to breathe deeply and fight the panic. The air wasn't thin and she wasn't in total darkness, but her arms were trapped on either side of her head. For some reason, that position filled her with terror. A sweat broke out on her body and she almost panicked. She was at the point of kicking her feet and screaming when she caught sight of Curt.

Her heart went wild. He seemed to be just as they'd expected, upright with his arms over his head. She kicked the tile to let the men know she needed to stop. Her descent halted just as her fingertips touched Curt's. She kicked once for a few more inches and then kicked again.

Now she could touch his hair and his face. "Curt! Curt, please talk to me! You have to be all right!" she whispered desperately. She held the vial of salts under his nose and snapped it with trembling fingers. His head jerked, bumping her hand and knocking the vial down the shaft.

Maggie swore profusely, using every foul word she could ever remember hearing. She tried to raise her head for a better look at Curt, but all she could see was the thickness of his hair.

EIGHT

"Maggie?"

The sound of Curt's rough voice echoed loudly through their private prison. A sob rose from Maggie's throat and she began to tremble.

"What the hell?" Curt's voice was stronger as he regained consciousness and became aware of his predicament.

"You fell into a well shaft," she explained throatily.

"Damnit," Curt cursed, his breathing rough. "I remember. The air was thin. I must have passed out."

"Mike said the gas might have made you unconscious." She was panting with each breath. "Did you hurt your head?"

"I don't think so, but I'm sure as hell stuck."

Maggie held the leather strap with a death grip in the fingers of her left hand. "I have to get a strap around your shoulders so they can pull us out of here."

His arms were pinned close to her shoulders, so she knew Curt couldn't help her much. She said a silent prayer and then kicked her foot to have Mike and Rand lower her closer to him.

"Can you feel the strap?" she asked him.

Curt moved his fingers and felt the leather. "I've got it," he said when he had a firm grasp.

"Just hold on in case I lose it," she told him, her voice hoarse with tension.

Holding the strap with her right hand, she wrapped one end of it under Curt's left shoulder. He pressed his back to the wall and held it in place while she shifted her hand from his front to where the strap was locked behind his shoulder. They repeated the process on the other side of his body. When Maggie could grasp both ends again, she latched them to the hook on her harness. Then she breathed a ragged sigh of relief.

She was trembling violently and her head was throbbing painfully. For just a second, she allowed her head to rest against Curt's, drawing strength from him.

"Are you okay?" he asked gruffly.

"I'm fine, just light-headed. I need to lock my arms around you, and you need to get a tight grip on this harness I'm wearing."

Maggie managed to reach as far as his armpits. She grasped him as firmly as possible while he caught hold of her harness. When they were ready, she kicked the tile two times and they began the slow, painful trip upward.

At first Maggie feared that Curt's weight would rip the harness off her body. All the air was forced from her lungs, and every muscle in her body protested the punishment. She stifled a cry and Curt swore profusely.

The going got rougher when his whole body was dragged into the smaller cavity of the tile. His shoulders barely fit, especially since he was holding on to her arms.

"Hang on to my head or my hair," she suggested hoarsely.

"No." Curt refused to hurt her more.

Maggie didn't have the breath to argue, but she knew his arms were going to be raw from dragging against the rough tile. Halfway up to ground level, she thought she would surely be ripped in two if they didn't hurry, so she kicked wildly at the sides of the tile.

The next thing she knew, her ankles were being grabbed by big, strong hands. She felt the evening air enveloping her body an inch at a time. Then Curt's weight was being born by Ron and Pete. Rand unfastened the hook that kept him attached to Maggie. Another hook, attached to the saddle horn of Curt's horse, was unclipped, as well.

Mike stood her on her feet, but she swayed dizzily and he lowered her gently to the ground. He carefully brushed the hair from her eyes, stripped her of the harness and miner's light, then smoothed her dirty, torn clothing.

Maggie forced herself to breathe slowly and deeply until normal circulation returned to her limbs. The evening air felt wonderful against her overheated flesh. She heard Curt thanking the men, and everyone seemed to be talking at once. It all sounded garbled and distant until Curt's temper flared.

"Have you guys lost your minds?" he rasped gruffly. "Whose fool idea was it to send Maggie down in that breathless grave?" He paused only to draw in air. "I appreciate being hauled out, but hell, couldn't somebody have thrown me a rope instead of risking her life?"

Maggie allowed a little smile to lift her lips. She tasted her own tears and knew that reaction was finally setting in. Curt was all right. He was behaving like a wounded bear, but his rampage made her heart swell with happiness.

The other men tried to calm him with assurances that Maggie had been perfectly safe, but he wasn't convinced. As soon as he regained his strength, he limped to where she was resting.

His image was a little blurred by tears, but Maggie gave him a brilliant smile. "Give 'em hell, cowboy," she teased. She wanted to reach her hands out to him, but her arms felt like they were made of lead.

Curt came down on one knee and slipped his hands under her shoulders. She moaned when he pulled her into his arms, but then clung tightly. The tears continued to slide down her cheeks while she basked in the pleasure of being in his arms. The sound of his vibrant heartbeat overwhelmed her with relief.

The others gave them some privacy as they went about packing up all the gear. Rand radioed an all clear to Craig with a big thanks for his help. Pete volunteered to ride Curt's horse back to the ranch.

Curt stroked Maggie's hair and murmured softly to her, telling her how brave and strong she was. When her breathing finally returned to normal and her tears stopped, he pulled her gently to her feet.

"It's getting dark. You need to go home and take a hot bath," Curt told her as he guided her toward the Jeep.

"You need to see a doctor," she retaliated.

"I'm fine."

"You're limping."

"I just twisted my ankle. It's nothing serious."

"You're sure you didn't hit your head?"

"I'm sure. I just need a hot shower and a good night's sleep."

"I'll take Curt home and see that he's all right," Mike offered as they approached the parked vehicles. "I'll give you a full report when I come back to the ranch."

"You're not staying at the ranch tonight?" Maggie asked in concern. She didn't think he should be left alone.

"I'd rather stay at my house," Curt's tone discouraged any arguments.

Maggie was too tired to wage a verbal battle with anyone. She allowed Rand to lift her in his arms and set her gently in the passenger seat of the Jeep. Then he drove her slowly back to the ranch.

Maggie didn't utter a word of complaint when Rand lifted her again and carried her into the house. They were immediately surrounded by concerned faces. Rand assured everyone that both Maggie and Curt were going to be fine. He carried her down the hallway to her rooms.

Once inside her bedroom, Maggie mustered the strength to stand on her own feet. A glance in the mirror drew forth a moan of dismay, but she quickly averted her eyes.

Tara drew her a bath and laid out a nightgown, then stayed close while Maggie soaked in the tub. Geraldine and Mindi brought her supper as soon as she was ready for bed. When everyone was finally convinced that she was all right, they left her alone to rest.

The bed felt heavenly. Maggie sighed as she snuggled under the covers. Her weary muscles relaxed and her eyes drifted closed. Still, she didn't sleep until Mike had returned and assured her that Curt was fine. Then she slept deeply.

It was after two in the morning when Maggie woke. She was instantly wide awake even though it was pitch-dark in her room. She'd been sleeping since nine o'clock, and she didn't feel the least bit drowsy. She tried to go back to sleep for a little while, but couldn't.

She wondered how Curt was feeling. Was he sound asleep? Was he having bad dreams? Was he restless? Was he really all right? She hadn't gotten much of a chance to talk with him last night, and now she was filled with concern.

He could be having a delayed reaction to his fall. Maybe his head had been injured without them realizing it. Maybe he had a concussion. She wished he had seen a doctor. She wished Mike had spent the night at Curt's ranch. Then someone would be close if Curt needed help.

Maggie was out of bed and dressing before she had time to analyze her motives. She moaned and groaned as she pulled off her nightgown and donned jeans. Her body was scraped and sore, her muscles stiff. Pulling a sweater over her head was the most painful, but the pain eased as she stretched her stiff muscles and slipped into a light jacket.

She was going to Curt's to make sure that he was okay. She wasn't going to bother him or even wake him, but she wanted to see for herself that he was sleeping comfortably. She left Tara a note in case someone checked on her and found her missing. Then she turned off the light and left her room.

There was a back door she could use to exit this wing of the house. Maggie rarely used it, but tonight it came in handy. Her car started quietly, and she waited until she was headed away from the house to turn on her lights. Rand had given her a remote control for the front gates, so she didn't have to disturb anyone as she left the McCain ranch.

It took less than ten minutes to get to Curt's driveway. Maggie turned her lights off so that she wouldn't disturb him. She parked her car and entered the house as quietly as possible, saying a prayer of thanks that Curt hadn't locked his doors.

Once on his back porch, Maggie peeked through the window of the kitchen door, but couldn't see a thing. She opened the door and entered the kitchen, quietly closing the door behind her. A faint light gleamed from the living room, so she tiptoed through the doorway.

Someone had left a light burning in the bathroom. There were also embers gleaming in the fireplace, so the living room wasn't totally dark. Maggie saw Curt stretched out on the sofa bed. She inched closer, hardly daring to breathe. It suddenly dawned on her that she had no explanation for trespassing and invading his privacy.

The room was comfortably warm. The furnace was running, and Mike had built a fire. She added more logs to the glowing coals, then moved to Curt's side. He was breathing peacefully, and she breathed a little easier at the sight of him.

He was gorgeous, despite the scrapes and scratches marring his smooth, golden flesh. She loved him desperately, though common sense told her the feelings would never be reciprocated. Curt wouldn't appreciate the depths of her emotional commitment to him, but she could no longer deny the truth. At least, not to herself—not after she'd come so close to losing him.

Her fingers itched to touch him. She wanted physical proof that he hadn't been seriously injured. She wanted to feel his strength and caress his hard body. Most of all, she wanted to wrap her arms around him and hug him tightly.

She wouldn't do any of those things. She balled her fingers into tight fists and watched him sleep. The light from the bathroom softly illuminated his big body. His hair was tousled and gleamed brightly against his tanned face. His features were relaxed in sleep and even more strikingly handsome.

He had a blanket pulled to his waist, but the broad width of his bare shoulders made Maggie's lungs constrict. She ached to touch him, to feel his hard warmth. The wanting was physical, emotional, and all consuming.

Sometimes wanting wasn't enough. Maggie refused to force her attentions on Curt. She knew if she woke him he would respond in a normal male fashion. He would pull her into his arms and make love to her. A tremor of longing shot through her. As much as she wanted his loving, she didn't want it that way.

Maggie decided she'd have to be content with just watching Curt sleep. She didn't want to leave just yet, but she'd leave before daylight. For now, she'd pull a chair into the living room and stay close for a while.

She went to the kitchen and eyed the straight-back chairs with disgust. Then she remembered that some of her own furniture was stored here. She flipped on a light switch to illuminate the back porch, knowing the light wouldn't shine as far as the living room. One of her bentwood rockers was sitting beside some other furniture.

It seemed to take an inordinate amount of time to get the rocking chair to the living room without bumping

SASSY LADY / 129

any walls or making any noise, but Maggie accomplished her objective. She placed the rocker between Curt and the fireplace, then realized that it was going to squeak on the bare wood floor.

Another forage in her belongings produced a small rug. With it under the rocking chair, she could rock quietly. In a few minutes, she managed to get herself comfortably settled.

Curt battled to keep his breathing even. He'd awakened from a hellish dream just before he'd heard Maggie creeping into the house. He wasn't surprised at her arrival. Some elemental, untried instinct told him they needed to be together.

She'd saved his life. He didn't doubt it, though he knew she'd deny it. If not for her quick thinking and brave actions, he'd probably have succumbed to the lethal gases in that dark hole. Mike had described her tenacity and determination to rescue him, and he was shaken by her unselfish actions.

Nobody had ever worried about protecting him. He knew that Rand, Mike, and the others would do whatever they could for him, but it wasn't the same as having one special person who cared enough to risk her life. The thought of Maggie's courage made his chest tight with emotion—painful, unfamiliar emotion.

During his lifetime, plenty of women had insisted that they loved him. Some had ranted, raved, and demanded that he return their love. If Maggie had done the same, he might be able to harden himself against her.

She didn't make demands. She didn't rant and rave. She seemed as wary as he was, yet she continued to weave herself into the fiber of his being. She'd never told him that she cared for him, but she'd proven it in many ways. Her actions seemed to be speaking to a part of him where no voice could ever be heard, the very heart of him.

Curt's mind was still too groggy to cope with the weight of emotional complications. He was soothed by the sound of Maggie's breathing and by her proximity. When she grew quiet, he slept.

A couple of hours later, near daylight, her movements caused him to waken again.

Maggie had dozed, but she didn't want Curt to know she'd been here. She wanted to return to the ranch before she was missed. Just before dawn, she quietly took her chair and rug back to the porch.

She returned to the living room for one last look at Curt, then caught her breath. His heavily hooded eyes were open and locked on her. They pierced her with an intensity that sent a tremor through her body.

Maggie went hot all over. Curt's eyes told her that he'd been aware of her presence the whole time. There was no accusation or condemnation in his eyes, just a blazing fire that singed her soul.

"I was worried," Maggie whispered, mesmerized by the turbulent emotion in Curt's eyes. He looked at her with a raw desire that was beyond the physical.

"Come here," he commanded softly, shifting and throwing aside the blanket, inviting her to join him in bed.

Maggie trembled. Curt was naked except for his briefs, and his big, virile body attracted hers like a magnet. She'd never been more tempted in her life. She literally ached to touch him. She was desperate for his hard warmth, but she wasn't a fool.

She was in over her head, and she wasn't sure she'd

survive if Curt loved her then rejected her. Her eyes begged him to understand her reluctance.

"I just want to hold you," Curt swore huskily, coaxing her with his brilliant, unblinking gaze.

The words were hardly out of his mouth before Maggie kicked off her shoes and shed her jacket. She crawled into the bed and slid her arms around his waist, hugging him fiercely.

Curt moaned low in his throat. He covered them with the blanket, then wrapped his arms around her and buried his face in the fragrant softness of her hair. She was all woman. Her soft curves molded to his hard angles, and she felt wonderful.

Maggie caressed the firm, smooth skin of Curt's back and rubbed her face against the tight curls on his chest. She heard the violent pounding of his heart and felt her own matching its heavy rhythm. He was alive, unharmed, and all male.

"I've never been so scared in my life!" Maggie told him, a sob catching in her throat as she remembered the crushing fear she'd experienced when his life was in danger.

"I know," Curt soothed. He didn't want her to suffer any more from the experience they'd shared. "It's over. We're safe."

Maggie tilted her head and glared at him, her eyes sparkling with tears. "Don't you ever scare me like that again."

Curt grinned at her. She made him happy. He couldn't resist dropping a kiss on her pouting lips. "Why don't you stop giving orders and get a little sleep?"

Maggie's smile was so radiant that it made his chest tight. He pulled her closer and gently stroked her hair, knowing he was a fool to encourage such intimacy. He didn't want her to care too much. He had to make her understand that he wasn't capable of committing himself to a serious relationship.

The privacy of darkness and the intimacy they shared made it easier to tell her about an experience that was partly responsible for his lack of faith in his own emotional depth.

"I've known a few women, but I was never tempted to live with one until my final year in the army," he explained quietly.

Maggie stiffened slightly and her arms gripped him harder. She wanted to know what had caused him to be so wary of commitment, but she wasn't sure she had the strength to cope with a tragic love story.

"Her name was Sally. She asked me to move in with her. She assured me that she was willing to accept what I could give. She said she wasn't looking for love and devotion, just companionship and someone to warm her bed," he declared derisively.

"I guess she was satisfied for a few months, but then she decided she wanted more. She wanted marriage, a family, and vows of everlasting love."

"You didn't feel the same?" Maggie queried.

"No." Curt's tone was grim.

"What happened?"

"I came home one day and found her in a pool of blood. She'd slit her wrists."

Maggie gasped and looked up at him. "She wasn't . . . ?"

"No," Curt said, soothing her with his hands while he continued. "I got her to the hospital in time to save her. She lost a lot of blood, but she didn't die."

"She probably timed her attempted suicide to conveniently coincide with your arrival," Maggie surmised grimly, her jealousy overriding her compassion. "She wanted to scare you and make you feel guilty."

"She accomplished that."

"But not your undying devotion?" asked Maggie.

"She killed any feelings I had for her. She made me feel colder and lonelier than I'd ever felt in my life."

Maggie already knew that he'd had a lonely childhood. His girlfriend's attempt to manipulate him had backfired and had made him retreat deeper into himself.

"I'm sorry you had such rotten luck with your relationship," Maggie murmured against his chest, "but I'm not sorry you left her."

"I was never sorry, either," Curt replied quietly. "I don't have the capacity to feel what she wanted me to feel for her. I'm as hard as she accused me of being, and even colder than I was before I met her."

Maggie went very still. Now she understood why Curt felt compelled to share his past with her. He didn't want her to think that what they'd experienced tonight would change his feelings for her—or lack of feelings.

She slowly raised her head until her eyes locked with his. "If you're warning me not to care for you," she told him huskily, "then your warning is wasted."

Curt closed his eyes against the honest emotion he saw in Maggie's. He didn't respond, but pulled her closer and held her against his heart. He didn't want to argue or think about the consequences of caring, even a little.

Neither of them spoke again. Both were satisfied with being close to each other. Curt felt Maggie relaxing and knew when she finally succumbed to exhaustion. Then he allowed himself to relax and sleep.

*   *   *

The next time Curt woke, it was to the sound of Rand and Mike entering the house. It was broad daylight, and the two big men weren't even trying to be quiet.

Maggie had shifted in her sleep and turned her back to him, curling spoon fashion against his body. She felt soft and smelled sweet. His arms tightened around her protectively.

When Rand and Mike moved into his line of vision, he gave them a silent warning not to disturb her.

Mike wasn't very good at heeding warnings. He propped his big fists on his hips and scowled at them. "I guess I'm the next of kin here," he declared in a loud aside to Rand. "Do you think I should get a shotgun?"

For a moment there was total silence. Then Maggie surprised them all by responding without even opening her eyes. "I think you should go suck an egg," she told him tonelessly.

Mike and Rand laughed. Maggie knew Curt was amused, too. His arms tightened, and she snuggled closer to him.

"You wound me, Midget," Mike told her.

"Then protect yourself by leaving," she suggested.

"Such ingratitude," Mike scoffed. "We were genuinely worried about the two of you."

"We're appreciative," injected Curt. "Now leave."

Maggie giggled and wriggled closer to him, but she stilled her movements when she felt his very male reaction. Curt wanted to laugh, to shout his pleasure at having her close, and to kiss her breathless. Having her in his arms was agony and ecstasy. He wanted time alone with her, time to explore what was developing between them. The feelings he had for Maggie were unique and intriguing.

His breathing grew a little ragged. His body grew taut as blood rushed to his loins. He glared at Mike and Rand, but they ignored him with malicious delight.

"Can we assume it's safe to tell everybody at the ranch that the two of you are fully recovered from last night's accident?" Rand asked blandly.

"We're fine," Maggie assured him, but a shudder ran over her body at the reminder of last night. She wasn't ready to leave Curt yet.

"We hate to break up this cozy little twosome," Mike told them without a trace of regret, "but Geraldine sent over a picnic basket with sausages, eggs, and biscuits. If the two of you aren't hungry, Rand and I can leave and take it with us."

Curt's stomach growled, and Maggie smothered a giggle. They both glared at the intruders but sighed in resignation. As pleasant as it might seem, they knew they couldn't spend the day in bed.

By mutual agreement, they carefully untangled their limbs, gently stretching their sore muscles. Curt pulled the blanket off Maggie and helped her sit up.

"How about making yourself scarce while I get some clothes on?" he suggested lightly.

"Such modesty," taunted Mike, his eyes challenging his friend.

"Damned right," Curt responded. The clipped words and the gleam in his eyes, coupled with the fact that Maggie was fully clothed, were evidence that they'd shared the bed in a platonic fashion. He silently dared the other men to criticize Maggie's decision to come to him.

NINE

"I have to visit the bathroom," Maggie declared while smoothing her rumpled clothing and slipping her feet into her loafers. "Then I'll make some coffee and set the table."

Curt waited until she was out of sight and climbed from bed. His body hurt all over; partly from the accident and partly from the persistent ache of his arousal.

"I hope you two have already eaten," he groused. "Because I don't feel like entertaining company."

"Do you want us to get Maggie out of your hair?" asked Mike, tongue in cheek.

Curt shot him a look that could kill. "You could get me a clean shirt." He wasn't going to discuss his relationship with Maggie, but he definitely didn't want her to leave.

Mike made a quick trip upstairs to a room where Curt kept his clothes. Rand retrieved the pair of jeans that were lying beside the sofa bed. He tossed them to his friend.

Every muscle in Curt's upper body protested at the simple act of dressing. His skin was scraped raw in several places. Mike managed to find him a soft cotton shirt, but it still irritated the tender areas.

"How's the ankle?" Mike wanted to know.

"A little weak," returned Curt. "But I'll live."

"Glad to hear it," Rand injected. His tone was light, but his eyes revealed how worried he'd been. "You gave us a helluva scare, old buddy."

Curt's lips tilted in a grin. "Maggie's already warned me not to do it again."

"That's my midget," Mike announced in a tone guaranteed to carry to the bathroom. "You'd be wise to take her advice or she'll nag you to death."

Maggie was leaving the bathroom and heading toward the kitchen. She threw Mike a glance that told him she intended to ignore him. Her eyes shifted to and lingered on Curt. She gave him a warm smile.

"Your turn in the bathroom. I'll have breakfast on the table in a few minutes. Are they staying?" she asked with a nod in the direction of their uninvited guests.

Curt laughed softly and his eyes sparkled. Rand and Mike groaned about not getting any respect.

Maggie entered the kitchen, burying the memory of Curt's laughter deep in her heart. No man had ever played such havoc with her senses and her emotions. She wondered what new turn their turbulent relationship would take now.

Would Curt revert to his indifferent attitude once the emotional furor of the accident had faded? Would he crawl back into his shell and lock her out because she'd admitted to caring for him? Would he try to further their relationship on a physical level? That thought produced a thrill of anticipation, and a blush.

Once the coffee was brewing, Maggie opened the picnic basket Geraldine had packed. The appetizing aromas that wafted from the basket made her mouth water and her stomach growl.

"Time to eat!" she yelled, setting several warm serving dishes on the table. "Mike, are you and Rand eating?"

"You don't have to scream," Mike replied as the three men moved into the kitchen. "We've already eaten."

"A cup of coffee might be nice," Rand stated, "but we have work to do and we don't want to overstay our welcome."

Curt just grunted and sat down at the table. Maggie flashed Rand a smile as she moved effortlessly about the kitchen, collecting silverware and plates to set the table, then pouring juice and milk for her and Curt.

"You sure seem to know your way around Curt's kitchen," Mike declared suspiciously, his arms crossed over his chest. "I didn't know you'd ever been here before last night. You flatly refused to come with us when we brought your furniture."

Curt's eyes sought Maggie's and one brow arched in surprise at the last tidbit of information. "Know one kitchen, know 'em all," he drawled.

"I thought you were leaving," Maggie reminded her nosy cousin. "I hate to be rude and eat in front of you, but I'm starving."

"That's all right," Mike grumbled as he followed Rand out the kitchen door. "You go ahead and eat. We'll just go to work and try not to collapse from lack of nutrition."

" 'Bye, Maggie," Rand called from the outer door. "Curt, don't even think about coming to the ranch for a couple days. That's an order."

"That doesn't mean you won't be sorely needed, Maggie," Mike called to her as he followed Rand. "You'd better not stay too long. Everyone will worry, and I'm sure Geraldine needs that basket back this morning."

Rand held the door for Mike, then got in the last word before they both left. "You're on sick leave, too, Maggie. Tara and I can handle the office until you feel like working."

The room seemed abnormally quiet when they'd gone. Curt drank his juice, but his eyes never left Maggie's lovely, flushed face. "Mike's a bit protective of you, isn't he?"

"A bit?" Maggie retorted, finishing her juice. "My boyfriends never minded meeting my dad, but the big guy usually had them running for cover. He can be pretty intimidating when he wants to be. You're lucky, you can ignore him."

"Does that mean you consider me a boyfriend?" Curt teased as he helped himself to generous portions of Geraldine's breakfast fare.

Maggie filled her plate. She knew her blush was deepening, but she battled for a detached tone. "I've never thought of you as a boy at all."

The tone didn't lessen Curt's reaction to her words. He went hot all over and found it difficult to swallow. Their eyes locked and then they shifted their gazes back to their plates. By silent, mutual agreement, they ate their meal without speaking again.

When Maggie was finished eating, she took her dishes to the sink and poured coffee for Curt. He rose from his chair, opened a cupboard, and handed her a box of tea bags.

Maggie stared at the box, then up at him. He'd managed to shock her speechless again. Since Curt didn't drink tea and he rarely had guests, he had to have purchased the tea because she'd told him she liked it. The thought boggled her mind.

"After you and Mindi took me kite flying," Curt explained, lifting a finger to gently stroke Maggie's flushed cheek, "I told her you were welcome to come and visit me. I didn't want to be a poor host, so I bought some cocoa for her and some tea for you."

His deep, husky tone was washing over her like molasses. Maggie knew he wanted to make light of his gesture, but she was thrilled to know that he cared, for whatever reason.

"Thank you," she finally managed, accepting the box and setting it on the countertop.

Her body seemed to move closer to him of its own volition. When she was very close, she reached up and pulled his head toward hers so that she could give him a kiss.

The light, hesitant touch of her lips fueled Curt's hunger for more. He caught her hips in his hands and held her closer while their mouths slowly brushed, locked, parted again, and then met once more.

Maggie wrapped her arms around Curt's neck. She was thrilled by the tender exchange of kisses. Nibbling gently on his lips, she felt a shudder quake over his body, and curved herself closer to his hard form.

A low moan escaped Curt as he captured her teasing lips and pressed his mouth firmly against the softness of hers. His tongue darted out to tease the length of her lips, begging entrance that was swiftly granted.

It was Maggie's turn to moan when Curt's tongue slid into her mouth in a slow, sensual mating that stole her breath and made her knees go weak.

Curt pulled her fully against him, lifting her off her feet and holding her close to the throbbing heat of his arousal. She arched her hips against him and he groaned again.

He felt the pebbled hardness of her nipples pressing against his chest. She wasn't wearing a bra. The knowledge made his head light and made the blood pound through his body.

Maggie gently sucked on his tongue as it made a thorough study of her mouth. She locked her fingers in his hair and held his head in a firm grip. The rest of her body involuntarily rocked against his, and their moans mingled in their mouths.

Curt lifted her higher and released her lips. He dipped his head to her breasts, softly nudging her nipples with his nose, and then teasing them with his mouth. The tight buds were pushing against the soft fabric of her sweater. He gave them this full attention, tugging them gently with his teeth, and then soothing them with his lips.

Maggie's hands tightened on his head as shudder after shudder racked her body. "Oh, Curt!" she exclaimed raggedly. Hot spirals of electricity were shooting from her breasts to the very core of her. He was creating an ache that tightened her stomach muscles and encompassed her whole body.

"Curt!" she moaned with delight as his mouth continued to play with her throbbing nipples. Then she dragged his head up so that she could have his mouth again.

Curt took her lips with renewed fervor. He'd wanted

to be slow and careful with her. He didn't want to scare
her with his passion, but her frenzied reaction to his
caresses made him burn. He thrust his tongue between
her lips and simultaneously clutched her hips against
the pulsing hardness of his loins.

Before long, they were both gasping for air. Their
lungs were on fire as they fought for control. Curt
brushed kisses over Maggie's cheeks and throat while
he caught his breath.

He gently sucked the pulsing vein on her neck as she
squirmed against him. Her hands busily stroked his
head while she kissed his forehead, his jawline, and his
chin.

Curt slid a hand beneath the back of her sweater and
splayed it across her waistline. His lips homed in on
hers again while his hand ran up her spine to press her
closer.

Maggie uttered a startled gasp when his hand spread
over the bruised flesh on her back. Curt's eyes found
hers as he quickly shifted his hand back to her hips.
He slowly lowered her to her feet.

"Is your back really sore?" he queried gruffly.

"Just a little," Maggie countered, trying to regulate
her breathing.

"I don't think I thanked you for saving my life,"
Curt murmured, dropping his head to brush a kiss
across her lips.

"I don't want thanks," she countered, her eyes di-
lated with desire. "I just wanted you alive."

Curt gave her a sexy, intimate smile. "I'm very
much alive," he teased, grinding his hips against hers.
"Now let me see your back. I might have some ointment that will help."

Maggie fluttered her lashes coquettishly. "Really, Mr. Hayden, you are too bold!" she drawled.

Curt chuckled and turned her in his arms. He gently lifted her sweater to her neck, then sucked in a ragged breath.

"Curt?" Maggie queried hesitantly, when his laughter abruptly ceased.

He was quiet for a long time as his fingers gently skipped over her back and across her shoulders. When he still didn't say anything, she stepped away from him, pulling her sweater down to her waist.

"It can't be that bad," she challenged as she turned and got a look at his tormented expression. "I saw it last night and it was just a little red."

"You're black and blue all over. You look like you've been beaten," he rasped hoarsely.

Maggie was genuinely alarmed by his reaction to the bruising. "It barely hurts," she argued.

"You cried out when I touched you."

"I'd forgotten it until you touched me. I had my back against you this morning and it didn't bother me."

"Damnit, Maggie, don't argue with me," Curt snapped. His eyes lost their haunted look, but they grew chillingly cold, the anger directed at himself.

"You could be scarred for life. You could have had your ribs crushed. You could have had a lung punctured. I'm surprised that damned harness didn't crush you to death!"

Curt turned from her in his agitation, and Maggie laid a hand on his arm. "I'm perfectly all right, Curt! I've always bruised easily. It doesn't mean that I've suffered any permanent damage. I'll be fine."

"No permanent damage?" he repeated grimly, his mouth twisting cynically.

Maggie was chilled by the sudden change in him. She took a step backward, and he turned away again. When he went into the other room, she didn't immediately follow. She took a deep, trembling breath, then decided to clean the kitchen while he worked off some of his anger in the living room.

Curt attacked the sofa bed with a vengeance, swearing angrily as he worked. He slammed the mattress into the frame and then jerked the framework into the storage compartment. The cushions sailed into place like launched missiles.

Fool, fool, fool, his brain taunted him. He was a stupid fool to allow himself to care about anyone. Hadn't life taught him the price of feeling too much? Didn't he know that with the good emotions came the bad? That with the positive came the negative? The good ones tempted him, but the bad ones still threatened.

Curt stood in the middle of the living room and battled to control the turbulent emotions that raged through him. He could deal with the memories, the hard facts, but not the emotions. When he allowed himself to feel, he felt all the old rage and pain. He couldn't afford to feel anything.

"Curt?" Maggie spoke to him softly as she entered the room. He turned to her, his eyes blazing, and she hesitated. "Would you like to talk about it? I'm a good listener and I'd like to understand."

"Would you?" he ground out roughly, then dragged in a breath and ran his hand through his hair. He didn't want to take out his frustration on her. She, of all people, didn't deserve the abuse.

"I'm sorry," he told her, his body rigid. He was still fighting for calm. He knew he had to shake off the remnants of the painful, frustrating memories.

"Sorry for what?" she encouraged softly. "Sorry that I got a little bruised? It's not the first time in my life and it's not likely to be the last. I'm not sorry that I helped with a situation that could have become a disaster. I'd do it again."

Curt ran his hand through his hair again. He knew she meant what she said. He knew she didn't blame him, but he blamed himself. If she hadn't cared about him, she wouldn't have gotten hurt.

"Curt, those leather straps didn't even break the skin. I won't have any scars."

For an instant his eyes were glazed and focused inward, not on her. Maggie realized he was dealing with pain from his past that had been triggered by their present situation.

"Were you abused as a child?" she asked gently. That could account for his being such a loner and being reluctant to commit himself emotionally.

"Is that why you said I looked like I'd been beaten?" She was guessing, grasping at straws, but his reaction assured her that she'd touched on a sensitive subject.

Curt leveled a dead stare at her. His hands were balled into tight fists at his side. His jaw muscles clenched and unclenched. Maggie thought he was going to explode, or worse—manage to control all the anger and bury it inside himself again.

He finally spoke to her, his tone low and gruff. "My uncle was a big man. His favorite form of punishment was his belt."

Maggie paled and her heart ached. She'd known his past had been lonely, but she hadn't known it had been terrifying as well. "Did he beat you?" she managed to choke out.

"Until I was old enough to fight back," Curt told

her, battling the wave of fury that accompanied the memories. "When I got bigger and stronger, he started using his belt against my aunt and younger cousins. They were girls."

Maggie's chest constricted with the shared pain. She could imagine the guilt and frustration he must have suffered. It was no wonder he'd been stunned at the sight of her bruises.

"He only did it when he was mad at me, and never when I was at home. I'd hear the girls sobbing and see what he'd done to them. They told me he beat my aunt, but she never admitted it."

"What did you do?"

"I went to the authorities, but my aunt wouldn't testify against him."

"What happened?"

"They sent me to a foster home. I was afraid to leave the girls, but they kept in touch. They told me he stopped beating them after I'd gone. I guess he just hated me to the point of violence."

Maggie's breath caught in her throat. What a terrible burden to bear, she thought. She'd been surrounded by love all her life. That kind of hate and abusive behavior were hard to comprehend. She wanted to hug Curt, to ease the pain of the memories, but she knew he wouldn't appreciate any show of sympathy.

"Is that when you joined the army?" she asked him. Curt was pacing in front of the fireplace. Maggie moved closer and sat down on the sofa, her eyes following his restless movements.

"As soon as I was sure the girls were safe with him."

"Have you kept in touch over the years?"

Curt stopped pacing long enough to study Maggie's

lovely, concerned expression. He wondered what she must think of a background like his. It was a far cry from the sort of upbringing she'd had.

"I wrote for a while after I joined the service. I sent some money and gifts for a few years. Then the girls left home and I lost contact."

"You never went home again?"

Curt's eyes grew colder. "New York was never my home."

Maggie knew that he was closing a door in her face. He didn't like discussing his past. She was surprised and pleased that he'd volunteered as much as he had. She was just sorry that the sight of her bruises had brought back all his painful memories. She hoped he wouldn't allow the old wounds to destroy their developing relationship.

"Curt?" she tested, rising from the sofa and stepping closer to him. "You said you might have some ointment for my back." Her eyes challenged him to put it all behind him and concentrate on her, to let her help heal the wounds. She didn't want him reconstructing barriers between them.

He looked into her eyes for a long, breathless moment. The tension was palpable, the temptation hard to resist, but Curt turned away first.

"I'll take you back to the ranch. Geraldine is the expert on healing ointments."

Damn! Maggie closed her eyes. She breathed a deep sigh of disappointment. He was back in his protective shell and pushing her away again. She was tired of being pushed, pulled, and pushed again.

She had trouble dealing with yet another rejection, especially after spending the night in his arms. She was irritated by his dismissive attitude and the emotional roller coaster ride.

"That's it?" she asked, opening her eyes and glaring at him as he moved toward the kitchen. "Here's your hat, what's your hurry?" she clipped.

"You don't have to leave if you don't want to," Curt declared quietly, returning her angry glare with an expression of absolute calm.

Maggie felt like screaming bloody murder. She wanted to shatter his infuriating control. She considered attacking him physically, either in anger or passion. She wondered if either method would dent the wall he'd very deliberately resurrected between them.

"I think you're a cheat and a tease, Mr. Hayden," she challenged boldly, her eyes flashing in indignation.

Curt's facial muscles tightened visibly. His body stiffened and his hands balled into fists again, but he didn't say a word.

His silence and cold stare infuriated Maggie more. "What gives you the right to destroy what's growing between us?" she argued hotly. "Why do you think you can make love to me one minute and order me out of your life the next? I'm not a toy that can be played with, then cast aside. I have feelings, too."

Curt could handle her temper, but the hurt in her eyes and tone made him feel guilty, and angry. "I warned you that I'm not interested in a long-term relationship or in commitment," he defended hotly. "You're the one who refuses to accept that fact."

"I don't remember ever saying that I wanted a long-term commitment," she retorted sharply.

"What do you want?" he asked in a dangerously low tone as he moved within inches of her. "An affair with the local cowboy? Some wild, reckless memories to store in a mental scrapbook? I can give you plenty of those."

Maggie cursed herself for going hot all over. She couldn't deny the pull of attraction. She couldn't deny that she wanted the wild, reckless passion.

The question was, could she survive with only the memories and not the man's love?

"I don't want anything that I have to beg for," she snapped irritably. "If I just wanted sexual favors, I could get them from a dozen different men. If you can't give me a little honest emotion, then I guess I don't want a damn thing you've got to offer!"

Maggie started around him in a temper, but Curt grasped her arms and held her still. The thought of her with other men made him feel murderous. They were both breathing harshly, and their eyes locked in a battle of wills.

Maggie knew her anger and annoyance would swiftly fade. The tears would follow, so she didn't want to be anywhere near Curt when the pain and rejection surfaced.

"I'd rather you didn't touch me," she told him in a husky tone. He immediately relaxed his grip, and Maggie stepped away.

"I'll take you to the ranch."

"I have my car here," she reminded.

Spinning on her heels, Maggie snatched her jacket from the floor and headed for the kitchen. She grabbed Geraldine's picnic basket and left the house without a backward glance.

The hell with him, she fumed as she revved the engine of her car and pulled out of the driveway. She didn't need this kind of aggravation in her life. She loved her work and was beginning to feel like she belonged here. She wasn't going to let Curt ruin her newly found contentment.

The iron gates of the McCain ranch opened wide for Maggie as she punched in the entry code. A sob tore at her throat, but she forced it back. She wasn't going to give in to the pain of Curt's rejection. Anger was the best weapon against depression, so she decided to stay angry as long as possible.

Mike was coming out the front door of the house when Maggie parked her car. He took one look at her thunderous expression and knew she and Curt had argued. He wondered how deeply her emotions were involved.

"Hey, Midget," he said lightly, "I thought Rand told you not to worry about coming to work."

Maggie stifled the urge to throw herself into Mike's arms and tell him her tale of woe. He'd always comforted her through her emotional crises. But this time, she knew that even her big guy couldn't ease the pain.

"I want to work," she told him flatly.

Mike's brow creased in concern. "Wanna talk about it?" he asked lightly.

"Do you want to talk about Elaine?" Maggie challenged, and was swiftly contrite. Mike's normally ruddy complexion went pale.

TEN

"God! I'm sorry, Mike. That was a cheap shot. I'm in a foul mood and you didn't deserve that."

Maggie set the picnic basket on the porch and threw herself into his arms. She hugged him fiercely.

"It's okay," Mike told her, hugging her and stroking her hair. "You're hurting and I was being nosy."

"That doesn't give me the right to attack you." Maggie's apology was mumbled against his broad chest. "I'm sorry for lashing out like that."

"Apology accepted," he declared, tugging a lock of hair so that she was forced to look at him. He didn't like the wounded look in her eyes. "You didn't hurt me, you just took me by surprise."

Maggie studied his beloved features. He was such a wonderful, caring man. He deserved some personal happiness. Ever since she'd come to Oklahoma, she'd been begging him to listen to her news about Elaine.

It was easier to discuss his problems than her own. "Does that mean we can talk about Elaine?" she asked softly, her eyes never leaving his.

151

Mike gave her a brief smile and gently set her aside. He'd spent years trying to forget Elaine. He hadn't succeeded. He knew he didn't have the right to care, yet he still couldn't banish her from his mind.

"What do you want to discuss?"

The question was the first small sign he'd ever given Maggie that he would tolerate a discussion of his personal life.

"I had lunch with her when I was home last spring."

Mike walked to the edge of the porch and stared unseeingly across the barnyard. In his mind was an image of a tall, willowy blonde with big, sad blue eyes.

"How is she?"

"She's surviving."

"How's Darrin?" Darrin was Elaine's paraplegic husband.

Maggie moved to Mike's side and laid a comforting hand on his arm. "Darrin died right after Christmas last year. The doctors said it was a stroke. Elaine said he didn't suffer."

Mike's big body was coiled with tension. He had a bruising grip on the porch rail. Darrin and Elaine had been his patients. Darrin's physical condition was degenerative; the disease was terminal. It had been his job, as a psychiatrist, to help the couple cope with his impeding death.

Mike didn't look at Maggie and he didn't speak. She was one of the few people who knew how desperately he'd loved Elaine and that the bitter guilt he felt was the reason he'd abandoned his career. She told him about her meeting with Elaine.

"I asked her if she had notified you. She said she'd wanted to, but she didn't think it would be right. She knows you have a new life here and she wants you to be happy."

"What's she doing?"

"She went back to school and earned a degree in nursing."

That surprised and pleased Mike. He'd advised Elaine to pursue a career. Darrin had been enthusiastic and supportive of the idea, but Elaine hadn't wanted to spend so much time away from him.

"She told me you probably wouldn't believe it, but that your advice helped them accept and prepare for the inevitable changes. They both felt indebted to you for your insight."

Mike's grunt of response was disbelieving. He'd broken every professional rule in the book. He'd fallen in love with a dying man's wife and made all their lives more miserable.

Maggie laid her head on Mike's shoulder, offering understanding and support. "You need to go home, big guy. You need to see her or you'll never be really free of the past."

Mike wasn't sure he wanted to be free of Elaine or the love they'd shared. He didn't think he could bear to risk being totally rejected. She'd clung to him in a time of deep emotional need. He'd fallen completely in love. Her emotions had been tangled with shame and guilt. Her love and respect for her husband had prevented her from giving her heart to another man.

"Is there anyone else in her life?" The question was dragged from the depths of Mike's soul.

"I don't think so. She said she's become a workaholic."

Mike's thoughts were turbulent. Elaine was free now, but he wasn't sure he had the courage to face her. She might not want him. He would be a reminder of all the pain and grief.

When he was quiet for too long, Maggie hugged him and told him more about her meeting with Elaine. "She looked as lovely and elegant as ever. She seemed calm, composed, and self-assured, but she still managed to pick my brain of every tiny detail about you."

A shudder coursed through Mike, then he forced himself to wipe all thoughts of Elaine from his mind. He turned to Maggie and gave her a bear hug.

"I think you and I need a break. Maybe we should plan a party or a night on the town."

Maggie smiled. The subject of Elaine was closed again, but at least she'd managed to impart a few important facts.

"What town are we going to have a night on?" she responded lightly.

"Lawton, of course."

"Of course?" she queried. She didn't think there was any place to party in Larson.

"There's a lounge where we go on Saturday nights. It's not the best place to take a woman, but you'll be safe with me."

"A lounge?" Maggie wasn't convinced.

"A bar and lounge," Mike insisted, grinning.

"In other words, a dive?"

Mike laughed and hugged her again. "Just be ready to go by eight. Don't worry about the details. I'll take care of you."

"You always have." Her tone conveyed a wealth of love.

"Yeah, but you're getting too good at manipulating me. That was a shrewd change of subjects."

"I learned from the best," she teased, her eyes sassy.

"So what happened at Curt's?"

Maggie's expression sobered. "He touched a spot on my back where that harness left bruises."

"And he's blaming himself," Mike surmised. "Nobody was at fault, unless you want to blame some dead well drillers."

"I know, but there's no reasoning with him."

"I told you that he wasn't an easy man to understand."

She understood. Every time Curt had allowed himself to care for someone, they'd suffered. His parents had died, his cousins had been abused, and his girlfriend had felt driven to attempt suicide. It wasn't a good track record for relationships. He'd erected an impenetrable shield around his heart.

"I think you're right about that night out," Maggie finally replied. "I'm going to get some work done this morning, but I'll take the afternoon off to pamper myself a little. I'll be ready to party by eight."

"Good girl," said Mike. "Rand's in the office with Tara. Will you tell him I'm just getting headed toward the barns?"

"Sure," Maggie agreed, parting ways with her cousin as she entered the house and moved toward the office.

She found Rand and Tara in the office, but they weren't working. They were locked in each other's arms.

Maggie started to turn away and leave them some privacy, but Rand spoke to her as he slowly released his wife. "There's no need to leave. I told Tara I had to get busy, but she just won't take no for an answer," he teased, his eyes gleaming wickedly as Tara shifted out of his arms.

"That's a bold-faced lie," Tara declared huskily. "I was just sitting at the computer, minding my own business, when he attacked me. I didn't have any choice but to cooperate."

Rand threw his hands up in feigned innocence. His eyes challenged Tara boldly and his tone was laced with amusement. "I never would have attacked you if you hadn't looked so restless and uncomfortable behind that computer."

Tara grunted indelicately and turned her full attention to Maggie. "For some reason, it drives my husband crazy to watch me at the computer. I think I'd better turn it over to you if you're sure you feel like working today."

"I'm fine," Maggie assured them both as their attention turned completely to her.

"It is Saturday," Rand reminded. "You don't have to worry about working."

"I was just going to catalog some invoices and then I promise to take the afternoon off. Would you tell Geraldine not to worry about me for lunch or supper? I'll fix something in my room."

"I'll tell her. I'm headed to the kitchen now," said Tara as she moved to the door with Rand. "Don't hesitate to raid the refrigerator if you want anything."

"Thanks," Maggie replied, "but I have plenty of food in my own kitchen." She smiled as the two left the room, still teasing each other.

Her smile turned a little sad as she seated herself behind the computer. Rand and Tara were so very much in love, and they made no attempt to hide their feelings.

Love radiated from them any time they were together. Maggie felt incredibly envious.

Tara had explained that their marriage hadn't been a bed of roses. She and Rand had been separated for nearly two years. Finding the courage to come home had taken Tara a long time, but she was the first to admit that Mindi, Rand's love, and their marriage had been well worth fighting for.

Maggie asked herself if her love was worth fighting for. She couldn't force Curt to return her love. If he didn't feel as much for her as she did for him, there was no sense in going to battle over a lost cause. Curt might never be willing to accept the love she ached to give him.

From the sketchy details she'd ascertained about his early life, she didn't imagine he had much experience accepting or returning love. He'd never learned how to be spontaneous and uninhibited with his emotions.

She decided that the only thing she could do was wait. Patience wasn't one of her virtues, but she didn't have much choice. Curt had shown her that he could be tender and sensitive. He might not think he had the capacity to love, but she knew he cared for her. What she didn't know was how much he cared or if his feelings were as strong as hers. All she could do was love him, regardless of how difficult he made that task.

Later that evening, Maggie brushed her freshly washed hair and swept it into a topknot, leaving a few curls around her face and neck. She'd decided to wear a dress for her night out on the town with Mike.

She had a closet full of dresses, but she hadn't worn them much since she'd come to work at the ranch. Tonight she chose one of her favorites that she considered casually elegant. They might be headed for a dive of a bar, but she still had the right to look nice.

The dress was teal blue with a cowl neckline. The soft wool knit had long, full sleeves with narrow cuffs. The hem brushed Maggie's knees and the fabric molded her figure lovingly. A silver, chain-linked belt accented her tiny waist.

Mike gave a long, low whistle when he greeted her. "Wow, do you look great in that dress," he complimented.

Maggie curtsied playfully, then handed him her coat so that he could help her into it.

"Thank you, kind sir. I hope I'm not overdressed for this lounge you're taking me to."

"The lounge could use a little class," he told her as he ushered her to his car. "But I'll probably have to spend the night fighting off love-struck drunks."

Maggie laughed softly. She was never worried about going anywhere with Mike. There were few men, however amorous, who wanted to challenge her big escort. She'd only seen him fighting mad a couple of times, but she didn't blame men for backing down when he threatened them.

The trip to Larson was short. The bar, when they entered, was much like any other small-town bar: smoke filled, noisy, and dimly lit. Maggie didn't mind. She was feeling a little restless and reckless.

Mike helped her out of her coat and hung it near the door while their eyes adjusted to the lighting. They heard a shout of greeting from the other side of the room. The place was crowded, but Ron Sheperd and Pete Davis waved them to their table.

The ranch hands were sharing one vinyl seat of a booth. She and Mike were beside the table before Maggie realized that Curt was seated, alone, on the opposite side of the table.

Her heart skipped a beat at the sight of him. He was dressed in his usual cotton shirt and jeans, but the royal blue plaid of his shirt deepened the blue of his eyes and emphasized his bronzed good looks. The lantern above his head made his hair look silver. The cool, steady look he gave Maggie made her lungs constrict.

Before she realized what was happening, Mike had scooted her into the seat next to Curt and squashed her between the two of them. She heard Curt's breath break when she was crushed against him and heat rushed over her with the force of a tidal wave.

"Mike, this seat's a bit crowded," Maggie complained, trying not to get scalded by the heat of Curt's body.

"The whole place is always packed on Saturday," he countered, motioning for a waitress. "You're so little that you don't take up much space."

Nothing short of a temper fit was going to get Maggie out of her predicament, so she decided to relax and enjoy being close to Curt. If he didn't like it, she thought, he could throw a fit.

Curt shifted, turning sideways to allow her a little more space. He put his left arm along the seat behind Maggie and let her settle more comfortably, even though her every movement rubbed his nerves raw.

He cursed Mike, Maggie, and himself for the enforced physical contact after having spent most of the day convincing himself that his desire for her would die a natural death if he ignored it. He'd seriously considered finding another woman tonight who could ease his frustration, but the idea hadn't held any real appeal.

"Is that better?" he asked, trying to give her a little breathing room.

Maggie dared to look directly into his eyes and nearly got singed for her efforts. Curt didn't disguise the wave of desire that washed over him when her body was forced more fully against his side.

Her right shoulder was tucked under his arm, and their thighs were touching from hip to knee. Fire coursed through Maggie's veins, both from the intimate contact and the heat of Curt's gaze. His features tightened grimly, and she knew it was due to the vulnerability of her expression.

A waitress appeared and gave them all a big smile. Mike asked Maggie what she wanted to drink and she ordered a rum and cola. The waitress managed an extra wide smile for Curt.

"You want me to freshen that beer, honey?" she drawled.

"No, thanks," Curt replied, painfully aware of Maggie's softness and warmth. He'd planned on getting rip-roaring drunk tonight, but her unexpected appearance changed his plans. He could barely control himself around her when he was sober. He didn't dare weaken that control.

Mike ordered whiskey. Maggie shot him a surprised glance. Her cousin rarely drank hard liquor. The last time she could remember was before he left Chicago for Oklahoma. He'd drunk himself into oblivion, hoping to forget Elaine. Maggie didn't know if the method had worked, but she knew he wasn't easy to handle when he was intoxicated.

"Are we getting smashed out of our minds tonight?" she asked him lightly.

"I am," came Mike's clipped response. "You'd better take it easy, though. You're the designated driver."

"I don't remember taking a vote," she retorted.

"It was unanimous." Mike's tone was unusually grim and Maggie dropped the subject.

When the drinks came, Mike rested both his arms on the table and got into a heated discussion with Pete and Ron about pro football. It was apparent that he didn't feel like conversing with her, so Maggie tried to relax and study her surroundings. It wasn't easy.

The entire right side of her body was being scorched by the heat of Curt's. From shoulder to thigh, she was locked against his hard form. She tried to ignore the heavy cadence of her heart, but had little success.

"Do you come here often?" Maggie finally managed a calm, casual tone.

Curt tilted his head closer to hear her question, and her pulse fluttered. She berated herself for the silly reaction.

"This is the only decent bar in town."

Which didn't really answer her question, thought Maggie, but she wasn't going to split hairs. At least Curt was speaking to her. She wondered how angry he was about their earlier disagreement.

Curt had spent the day trying to convince himself that Maggie was just a passing fancy. He'd wanted other women. He'd decided that the intensity of his reaction to her was a result of his instinctive knowledge that he couldn't have her. Loving her would be like playing with dynamite. Why risk it? In a few months, she'd be gone, and he'd be alone again.

She was sweet, kindhearted, and incredibly desirable, but so were a lot of other women. He could resist temptation.

At least, he'd been sure he could, until she'd slid into the seat and shifted close enough for him to feel her softness, smell the sweetness of her scent, and hear the musical tone of her voice. He ached with a primitive pain that was totally new and beyond the physical. It was going to be a long night.

Maggie racked her brain for the casual conversation that usually came so easily to her. She sipped her drink and tried to think of a safe subject for discussion. None came, so she decided it might be safer to listen to Mike's defense of his favorite football team.

"The Bears will come on strong this year."

"They're washed up. I told you that last year, and I was right," argued Ron.

"They have the talent. They just need to get their act together," Mike insisted.

"They're a bunch of wimps," Pete dared. "The Forty-Niners stay healthy and get the job done."

Mike roared his dislike for San Francisco and ordered another drink. Then he began to argue about coaching problems. Everyone knew the list of options would be lengthy.

Ron was more than happy to continue the argument, but Pete just grunted. He gave Maggie a smile. "I know you don't want to hear this garbage. The band's playin' a slow one. Would you like to dance?"

Curt tensed beside her. Maggie knew if she danced with Pete that she'd probably end up dancing with every man in the place. The alternative was staying locked by Curt's side. She decided she needed more space.

"I'd like that, Pete," she told him with a smile. "Do you think we can convince Mike to let me out of here?"

Mike heard her, grunted, and stood up to let her slide

out of the seat. He took a long swallow of his drink and kept right on arguing football.

Maggie let Pete usher her to the dance floor. It was only big enough to accommodate a half dozen couples, but it didn't matter because all they did was shuffle around in a small circle. As soon as the song ended, Pete was tapped on the shoulder by another of McCain's employees, and Maggie spent the next hour being passed from partner to partner.

She felt Curt's eyes on her as she adjusted to each man's unique style of dancing, but she didn't glance toward their booth. Curt was the only single man in the bar who didn't come forward to dance with her, and the knowledge rankled. She forced herself to smile, chatter, and pretend she didn't care.

One particularly persistent cowboy kept cutting in on the others and Maggie liked him the least. Most of her partners held her at a polite distance, but he kept trying to draw her closer with every dance. He was also getting very drunk.

Over the din of the music, she learned that his name was Jock and he worked for Craig Sanderson. He was very handsome, conceited, and more obnoxious each time she danced with him.

Maggie was trying to discreetly pry herself from his arms when she saw a large hand slap his shoulder. It wasn't exactly a polite tap of interruption. Jock immediately released his grip on her and became belligerent.

Maggie's eyes flew to Curt's. They were murderous. She didn't know how often fights erupted in this place, but she refused to be the cause of a free-for-all. She swiftly pressed herself against Curt's chest and slid her arms about his neck, effectively changing partners before Jock could protest. Another couple nudged him out of the way and Maggie sighed with relief.

Curt's arms tightened around her. Once Jock was off the floor, his eyes met hers, but his feet never moved.

Maggie gently swayed to the music. "Are we going to dance?"

"I can't dance," he told her.

She shifted her eyes from his, thinking he just didn't want to dance with her. "Can't or won't?"

"Can't," clipped Curt, tightening his hold as she continued to rock back and forth in time to the music.

Maggie temporarily forgot her annoyance and remembered that he'd never flown a kite, never learned how to play, and probably had never learned to dance. She dared a glance at him from beneath her long lashes.

"If you can walk, you can dance," she contended. "I know you like music. You're probably just too contrary to try."

Curt felt some of the tension uncurl from his body, being replaced by the sharp sting of desire. He was crazy about her sassy mouth. And all the rest of her.

His hard warmth made Maggie's knees go weak and it irritated her. She stared into his eyes and wondered why he had to be the man who made her pulse run rampant and her body tremble. Why did he affect her this way?

She'd danced with more than a dozen men tonight. They'd all been eager to please her, and more than anxious to get to know her better. Curt didn't want anything to do with her, yet her body went wild at the feel of him. It just didn't seem fair. What made him so sexy and appealing? Why couldn't she care about someone who would appreciate her interest?

"What are you thinking?"

Maggie didn't realize she'd been staring into Curt's eyes for an unusually long time until she was snapped out of her reverie by his gruff question.

For an instant, she was tempted to blurt out her thoughts; but for once, she resisted the urge. She shifted her gaze and changed the subject.

"Do you think you could get us across the floor toward the ladies' room and then stay close until I make it back to the table?"

Curt didn't like the way she ignored his question and effectively closed him out of her thoughts. He was used to candor from her, but he couldn't force her to talk to him.

Keeping one arm securely about her waist, he led her from the floor, discouraging anyone who tried to intercept them.

When they were back at the booth, Maggie was once again crushed against his hard length. The waitress brought her a fresh drink and she downed it thirstily, trying to ignore her body's feverish reaction to the feel of him.

"Why didn't you rescue me about twenty dances earlier?"

Because he'd been battling a jealousy that knotted his gut and made him see red. It was a unique, unpleasant, and unwelcome experience. Curt hadn't been sure he could handle the raging emotion without violence. He'd wanted to rip Jock Carter's head off his shoulders.

"You were safe enough until Jock had too many beers. He thinks he's a ladies' man and he's a nasty drunk."

Maggie gave her full attention to her empty glass. The rum had hit her stomach with a vengeance, making her feel a little queasy. So much for drowning her sorrows. Her stomach always revolted before the rest of her could get numb.

"Another drink?" Mike asked, waving to the waitress.

"No, thanks."

"Curt?"

"I've had enough."

"A couple of real party poopers," Ron accused.

"Actually, I think I'm ready to call it a night," Maggie told them while she had Mike's attention.

"It's just past ten," argued her cousin.

"Yeah, but she's had a pretty rough week." Pete reminded them all of the accident yesterday.

"I'll drive myself home," she told Mike. "I'm sure Ron and Pete will let you ride back to the ranch with them."

"I'll take you and come back," Mike said, sliding out of the seat. He was followed by Maggie, then Curt.

"I'll take Maggie home. I'm calling it a night, too," said Curt.

"Maybe she doesn't want you to take her," growled Mike in a belligerent tone. The large amount of alcohol he'd consumed was altering his normally congenial behavior.

Maggie stiffened and so did Curt. The two men glared at each other like angry strangers instead of best friends.

"Maybe you're too drunk to drive," Curt challenged.

Maggie looked from one big man to the other. Their eyes gleamed with the light of battle. Their posture was rigid, their hands balled into fists. They were both itching for a fight. Men, she thought in disgust, why did they have to be so juvenile?

"I'm perfectly capable of getting myself home," she injected irritably, but was ignored by both men.

"Maybe Maggie prefers a drunk chauffeur to an amorous one," Mike taunted.

Curt's hands came up and he made a move toward Mike, but Maggie quickly stepped between them. She pressed herself against Curt's chest, just as she'd done when they were dancing. It took all her strength to halt his aggressive movement.

"Stop this right now! You're not going to use me as an excuse for a stupid fight! I won't have it!"

Curt glared at Mike over her head. Mike was mumbling insults, and the tension between them heightened.

"Do you hear me?" she insisted, raising her voice, then turning angry eyes on Mike. "Do you hear me? No fighting!"

It suddenly dawned on the two men that Maggie was clinging to Curt. She wasn't looking to Mike for a champion, but concerning herself with Curt. Her instinctive action spoke louder than words.

Curt suddenly lost all interest in fighting and forgot Mike. His eyes locked with hers for a long, intense moment. "Do you want me to take you home?" he asked quietly.

"I would appreciate that," she responded while putting some distance between them.

Mike's stance relaxed. "You sure you don't mind riding with him?" he asked. "I can call it a night if you want me to take you."

Maggie eased farther away from Curt, but his eyes held her captive. She knew she could drive herself home, but she wanted to be alone with him. She called herself every kind of fool, yet she agreed to ride with Curt.

"You can stay and party," she told her cousin. "Just

try not to start any brawls, and let someone else drive you home, please.''

"I'll be on my best behavior," Mike promised without conviction. He abruptly forgot them and became more concerned about getting a refill for his drink.

Maggie shook her head and frowned. She had a feeling Mike would be involved in an all-out brawl before the night was over. Probably with Jock, since the two of them were drunk and leaning toward disorderly.

Curt grasped her elbow lightly and led her toward the door, then helped her into her coat. Maggie was dismayed when she heard Jock's voice call out to them.

"You're not going home are you, sweetheart? The night's young and you're the prettiest little lady we've seen around here for a long time." His tone was a slurred whine.

Maggie forced a smile and deliberately placed herself between Curt and the approaching cowboy. "I'm really tired tonight, but maybe I'll come back sometime."

"Don't encourage the bastard," hissed Curt.

"I'm trying to discourage him," she hissed right back.

"Then tell him to go to hell."

"Good night, Jock," Maggie said quickly. She grabbed Curt's hand and hurried out the door.

Curt said something over his shoulder to the other cowboy, but she didn't hear it. She just wanted to get out of the bar and breathe some fresh air. She was tired of macho males and their ego battles.

ELEVEN

The night air was crisp and reminded Maggie of autumn in Chicago. So far, the Oklahoma weather hadn't been nearly as cool as November at home. It was hard to believe that Thanksgiving was just a few days away.

She wondered if Curt ever missed the season changes of New York, but she didn't ask. He was quiet as he showed her the way to his truck, and she didn't break the silence.

They were halfway to the ranch before she dared to look at him. His features were tightly controlled, and he stared at the road without a glance in her direction. The tension between them was palpable.

Maggie wanted to break the silence, but couldn't find the right words to say. She couldn't think clearly. All she could do was feel, and the feelings were painfully intense.

When they were nearing the turnoff to Curt's ranch, Maggie knew she'd have to do or say something to shatter his fierce control. If she didn't make the first move, Curt would drive past his house and take her straight to the McCains'. She had to let him know how she felt.

Sliding across the seat, she closed the distance between them and boldly turned toward Curt, laying her right hand lightly on his thigh. The strong muscle beneath her palm jerked, and the truck lurched. His reaction spurred her to more boldness.

"I don't really want to go home," Maggie whispered very near his ear.

The warmth of her breath caused a chill to course over his body, but it didn't cool the white-hot fire of her touch on his thigh. Nothing could diminish the primitive passion induced by her softly spoken words. Curt was aching, and more tension spiraled through his body.

He slowed the truck, pulled into his driveway, then came to a stop near the back porch. He shut off the ignition and turned to Maggie. Their eyes locked, their features barely visible in the pale light of the moon.

Curt's voice was rough and hoarse when he finally spoke. "If I take you into the house, I'm going to spend the rest of the night exploring every inch of your body with my body, my hands, and my mouth. I won't be easily sated and I'm not sure I can be gentle. Once we're lovers, a platonic friendship is out of the question." He paused briefly. "Be sure this is what you want."

Maggie carefully studied his tight features from the hard muscles of his jaw to the taut line of his lips. His body was rigid with tension. He hadn't made a move to touch her, and she knew it was taking all his considerable strength to keep his desire in check.

He was trying to warn her, yet again, that he wasn't

an easy man to love. She might have been put off by his harsh attitude if he weren't looking at her with eyes so hungry that they made her toes curl and her blood run hot.

Maggie wanted to shatter his control. She wanted him as weak and helpless with desire as she was. She didn't want him to have any doubts about making love to her.

Her eyes remained locked with his while she slowly slid her hand up his thigh. She hadn't thought his eyes could get any darker with need, but they did. His body bucked as she continued to explore the blatantly male shape of him through the denim of his jeans.

Curt's moan was low and tortured. By the time Maggie's wayward caress slid over his stomach to his chest, his blood was raging through his veins, scalding him, scaring him. Instinct urged him to drag her over his lap and sheath himself in her.

All remaining semblance of sanity told him she wasn't as experienced as her bold action suggested. She was teasing and testing her ability to arouse him. He knew she'd be shocked and hurt if he let his passion rage out of control, taking her callously on the front seat of his truck.

He slid from beneath the wheel toward Maggie. When he had more room to move, his let his hands rest lightly on her shoulders. He trapped her slim body between the seat and his own body. Only then did his eyes leave hers, and they only drifted as far as her mouth.

Maggie was melting. She couldn't have moved if her life depended on it. She was dragging in panting little breaths, her chest was heaving, and her nerves were raw. She wanted Curt's mouth as she'd never wanted anything in her life.

When his lips finally touched hers, Maggie was almost paralyzed with need. Her limbs were heavy and she couldn't seem to move, but Curt's mouth gave her sustenance. His tongue flickered along her lips, not quite kissing, but gently wooing. Maggie was sure she would die of wanting.

Curt let his mouth wander over her delicate features: the silk of her lashes, the curve of her cheeks, the tender underside of her chin. She was so soft. She smelled sweet and sexy. He wanted to taste.

His hands cupped her face and he brought her mouth close to his. His tongue teased her lips, begging entrance. Maggie's mouth opened on a broken sigh, and Curt locked his lips with hers. Their heads tilted for closer contact, and soft moans mingled.

His mouth was firm and hard, yet gentle. Their tongues tangled; hers teasing while his tenderly explored. He was being incredibly slow and thorough in his investigation of her mouth.

Maggie wanted more, faster and harder. She began to suck greedily on his tongue, urging him to ease some of the restraint he was displaying. She'd waited too long to go so slowly. She couldn't stand it. When Curt eased his lips from hers, she cried out in frustration.

"Curt!" It was a breathless plea.

"I don't want to hurry," he told her gruffly. "I want to enjoy every second."

One big hand still cradled her face, but the other went to the back of her head and slowly began removing pins from her chignon. His eyes didn't stray from hers until he'd freed her hair. Then he combed his fingers through the heavy tresses, brought a handful of hair to his face, and rubbed the textured silk against his lips.

"So beautiful," he told her in a barely audible whisper.

His husky words energized Maggie. She slid her hands under his jacket and locked them behind his back, squeezing him tightly, and pressing herself closer to his chest. She strung kisses over his neck, throat, and chin. Eyes closed, she blindly searched for his mouth and was rewarded by the heat of another long, exploratory kiss.

Curt thrust his tongue into the warmth of her mouth. A shudder ripped through him as she sucked it hungrily. Blood surged through his veins like liquid fire, making him hotter and harder than he'd ever been in his life. She was driving him crazy with nothing but kisses.

He was fighting for control and Maggie was battling to shatter his control. Curt's mouth grew more insistent, his lips and tongue demanding. He wanted her to feel the same frenzied desire that was burning him alive.

He wanted to pull her into his lap and strip away the layers of clothing that separated her softness from his hardness. He wanted her naked, in his arms, riding his hard body to completion. But he wanted more, so much more.

Easing out of her arms, Curt dragged in a calming breath and then got out of the truck. He strode quickly to the passenger door. The activity and cool air helped him regain some rapidly disintegrating control. It lasted until he was lifting Maggie out of the truck and she wrapped her arms around his neck.

When her lips homed in on his again, another tremor shot through his body. He wanted to carry her into the house, but first he had to return her kiss and show her how much he loved the taste of her.

Maggie let her body slide heavily against him while he closed the truck door. Then she was demanding his full attention with her small probing tongue darting in and out of his mouth.

Curt groaned, and stilled her teasing by sucking her tongue more deeply into his mouth and grinding his lips against hers until her head was pressed backward against his shoulder. Then he released her mouth and swung her into his arms.

Maggie clung tightly, loving the strength of the arms holding her. She could feel the pounding of his heart against his chest, and hers beat a matching rhythm. She'd never known such heady excitement. Her senses were reeling. She'd wanted Curt to lose control, but she was thrilled by his restraint.

He carried her through the porch door, stood her on her feet long enough to shrug out of his coat, help her off with hers, and lock the door. Then she was swept into his arms again and carried through the kitchen.

When they entered the living room, Curt stopped to flip on a light switch. Maggie blinked at the sudden brightness and he pressed kisses on her eyelids.

Her heart soared. His simplest actions were giving her the greatest pleasure she'd ever known. Curt was an incredibly sensual man and she wanted to sate herself with his sensuality. She knew he was growing increasingly impatient, and she suddenly wanted to slow down their time together.

Maggie eased herself out of Curt's arms, offering him only a seductive smile in explanation. She kicked off her shoes and turned to search the room. Finding the radio, she crossed the room and turned on his favorite station. It was time for love songs again, and Maggie's smile deepened.

"I want to dance with you," she told him softly, her eyes beckoning to him while her body swayed gently to the music.

She was so beautiful that Curt's pulse shifted into a higher gear. Her hair was tumbling over her shoulders in a riot of heavy curls. Her dress clung to all the slender but rounded curves of her slight form. He ached at the sight of her.

"I don't know how to dance," he reminded gruffly, while kicking out of his boots and pulling off his socks.

"I'll teach you," she promised, her eyes never leaving him for an instant.

Curt slowly unbuttoned his shirt, pulled it off his arms, and let it fall to the floor. Then he unfastened his belt buckle, slid it out of his jeans, and tossed it aside.

Maggie watched him, mesmerized. He was gorgeous: bronze, all brawn, utterly beautiful. The hair on his chest was almost silver, thick and curling to a point that disappeared at the waistline of his jeans. Her tongue flicked out to wet her suddenly dry lips.

"I want to dance," she reminded him huskily.

Curt didn't say a word. He moved toward her slowly, his eyes never leaving her lovely features. When he was close enough to touch her, he reached out and unclipped the belt of her dress.

It fell to the floor with a soft thud, and Maggie's heart thudded against her rib cage. Curt reached for the zipper of her dress and lowered it slowly. Next he gathered the hem of her slip and skirt in his big hands and pulled the clothing from her body. Maggie didn't utter a tiny sound of complaint.

"If we're going to dance," Curt told her while his eyes roamed freely over the sheer teddy she was wearing. "I want to feel you moving against me, skin to skin, no clothes in the way."

The boldness of his appraisal made her nipples tighten against the lacy fabric, and his eyes grew more turbulent with need. Maggie thought she might suffocate from her own agitated breathing. Then Curt unsnapped his jeans and stepped out of them. She trembled violently, fighting for breath.

When he kneeled in front of her, she grasped his shoulders for support. Her knees were weak, her bones had turned fluid. He didn't help by sliding his fingers under her stockings, releasing the catch on her garters, and slowly rolling the silk from her legs.

Maggie's fingers tightened on his bare shoulders, her nails biting into his hard flesh when he caressed the back of her legs with his big, rough hands before rising to his feet again.

"Oh, Curt!" she exclaimed raggedly as she clutched at his chest for support. Any minute she would melt.

"You wanted to dance, remember?" he teased gently, brushing kisses across her shoulders with enough force to shove the straps of her teddy down her arms.

"I want you to make love to me," she argued breathlessly, her fingers clinging to the firm, smooth flesh of his naked torso. Her hips arched toward him of their own volition.

"I want to dance with you," he countered, pulling her into his arms and drawing her so close to his body that they moved as one.

"I'm too weak to dance," Maggie murmured as she slid her arms around his neck and pressed closer to his hard frame.

"You're supposed to be teaching me," was Curt's reply. "One, two, three, turn," he commanded gruffly.

He felt a tremor course over her as their bodies swayed against each other in time to the sensual rhythm that filled the room. A shudder ripped through him as her hardened nipples were crushed against his chest. He wasn't sure how long he could sustain this sort of torture.

"I'm dying," Maggie complained passionately as Curt's hard body rocked against hers. "You're trying to kill me!"

"I just want you to have a little death." His response was so low that Maggie could barely hear it, but still it sent shudders over her body. She didn't understand.

"I'll explain sometime," he promised as he brushed kisses over her slightly parted lips. He wanted her satisfaction as much, or more, than his own. His desire was too fierce and would be quickly sated the first time he joined their bodies. Maggie wouldn't be satisfied unless she was totally aroused.

Arousing her gave Curt the greatest pleasure he'd ever known. She was so sweet, so sexy, and so trusting. He wanted to make love to her all night. He wanted to explore her passionate nature and drive her wild.

Maggie decided that she had to fight fire with fire. He wouldn't be rushed, so she had no qualms about launching a full-fledged attack. She started at his neck with her teeth and then gently nibbled her way down his chest to the tight male nipples buried in whorls of silver curls.

Curt's big body trembled and she smiled, then flicked her tongue over one nipple. When he groaned and grasped her hips in a fierce hold, she licked her way to the other nipple and bathed it thoroughly.

"So," he grated near her ear. "You want to play rough."

Maggie threw back her head and locked her eyes with his. This time the fire that blazed between them was almost too hot for either of them to handle.

"I think you'd better take me to bed before the fighting gets any rougher," she suggested throatily.

Curt wanted to kiss her breathless. He wanted to kiss every inch of her body. He wanted to bathe her nipples with his tongue, to suckle and nibble on them until she cried out in ecstasy. He agreed that he'd better not start until they were safely in bed.

Maggie laughed huskily when he swung her into his arms again. "No sofa bed tonight?" she teased.

"I have a brand-new bed," he told her, his eyes possessive as they roamed over her lovely, smiling features.

"I hope you're willing to share," she taunted as he climbed the stairs and carried her through the door to his bedroom.

Curt lowered her to the bed, but gently untangled her arms from his neck when she would have pulled him down with her. Maggie's eyes flashed in annoyance and he gave her a wicked grin. "You're too impatient."

When he stood beside the bed, she lifted a bare foot and ran it up his thigh. "And you're not?" she sassed.

His eyes flared as her caressing toes roved beneath the leg hole of his briefs and came intimately close to the rigid evidence of his arousal. God! She made his head spin and his blood boil. She would have to pay for the deliberate torture.

Grabbing her bare foot, he began to caress the sensitive curve of her instep with sure fingers. He watched as Maggie's eyes closed with pleasure, and treated her other foot to the same massage. Her low sounds of pleasure thrilled him.

Maggie couldn't believe how wonderful his touch felt. Tonight was the first time she'd worn heels in months and she'd been on her feet all evening. She hadn't realized how tired and sore she was until Curt's strong fingers kneaded the sensitive flesh, sending currents of erotic sensation up her legs.

Next, Curt's hands were sliding up her legs. He came down on the bed with a knee between her knees while his hands moved to cup her hips. He lifted her and slid her to the center of the bed, then continued to stroke her with his hands and mouth.

He rubbed his face over the silk of her teddy and then his lips found the straining peaks of her breasts. Maggie felt her whole body tightening as his mouth gently tugged on each nipple through the lacy fabric. She moaned deeply, clutching at his head and locking her fingers in the thickness of his hair. Her legs shifted and she squirmed restlessly.

When she began to whimper his name, shudders of primitive desire rocked Curt. His control was slipping again. He wanted her naked. He tugged the teddy off with help from Maggie. Then his breath broke at her exquisite beauty.

She was so small, yet so perfectly shaped. Her breasts were full and firm, with tight, dark nipples. Her waist was tiny, but her hips were rounded and her legs were gorgeous from thigh to toe.

Curt found himself gasping for air. Her passionate beauty clutched at his heart, making every breath more painful. For an instant, he was deeply afraid to touch her.

Maggie's lashes swept up and her passion-clouded eyes locked with Curt's. He was turned on his side toward her, but no longer touching her. She saw the turbulent emotion in his eyes and sensed his hesitancy. She splayed a hand over his chest, then let it drop to the waistband of his briefs. A gentle tug told him that she wanted nothing between them.

Curt shrugged out of the shorts, then turned to her again. He still didn't make a move to touch her, so Maggie stroked his cheek with the palm of her hand and then guided his face down to hers for a kiss.

Their mouths met and mated passionately. The hunger in them was insatiable. Their desire was soon raging out of control again as their tongues dueled ardently.

When they were gasping for air, Maggie clutched at Curt's head and guided his mouth to her breasts. She was soon moaning and writhing as his tongue bathed first one taut nipple and then the other.

She thought she would surely lose her mind when he sucked one nipple into his mouth while his fingers were playfully tugging at the other. She couldn't imagine a pleasure more intense, but Curt taught her more when his hand slid down her body and his fingers began a more intimate caress.

Maggie cried out in surprise, and Curt swallowed the series of moans that escaped her as his fingers stroked her most sensitive flesh.

She couldn't stand it. The pleasure was unbearable. It was too intense, too shocking, too new. Maggie dragged her mouth from Curt's, and looked into his eyes in feverish confusion.

He grinned at her, a slow, sexy, hungry grin. Her

reaction assured him that no other man had touched her as intimately. That pleased him more than he cared to tell her.

"I won't hurt you," he promised hoarsely.

"I'm already aching," she returned huskily. "Please make it better. Please."

Her sexy plea and the complete trust in her eyes sent a shudder over Curt's body. He was one big ache. She was one very small woman. He wasn't sure she could handle the length and strength of him.

"You're so little," he argued gruffly, his fingers verifying the fact with more intimate caresses.

Maggie was nearly out of her mind. She wanted him desperately. She grasped his arms and pulled him against her until his chest was rubbing against her throbbing breasts.

Curt's groan was deep and low as their mouths locked and he shifted his weight fully over her slender form. Maggie locked her arms around him and hugged him fiercely as she felt him fitting his hardness to her softness. He filled her, and she wrapped her legs tightly around his powerful thighs.

Damp, gripping heat. Curt had never been so hard, had never throbbed so hotly, had never been so tightly sheathed. His lungs ached with each tortured breath. His body was bathed in sweat. He was paralyzed with fear.

Maggie's satin thighs closed around him and he felt the ripples of her release the first time she arched herself closer to him. She cried out, he plunged deeper, and then his body was rocked by the fiery sensation of release. Shudder after shudder ripped through him.

Curt felt her taut nipples against his chest as he collapsed against her in exhaustion. Maggie's arms clasped him tightly as they both fought for breath.

"I had no idea," she finally managed to tell him. She'd experimented with sex once, but hadn't thought it worth the risk. Now she was stunned.

Curt raised his head so that he could look into her bemused eyes. His smile was warm, intimate, possessive.

He knew she wasn't very experienced. Her body and her reactions were evidence of the fact. He was elated that he'd provided her with her first real taste of passion.

"You're a very sexy, passionate lady," he told her.

"Is it always this way?" she asked. She was madly in love with Curt. That explained the intensity of her feelings. He'd been with other women. Had he felt the same pleasure with them?

Curt looked deeply into her eyes and understood what she was really asking. "It's never been like this," he swore, then feathered kisses over her cheeks.

"Really?" Maggie demanded. She wanted to believe that what they'd shared was rare and special.

"Really," Curt insisted with a roguish grin. "Nothing even compares." He'd never given so much of himself to any woman. He'd never wanted such complete loving with another woman. Maggie had brought out aspects of his nature that he hadn't known existed—sensitivity, tenderness, deep sensuality.

Her smile was wide and satisfied. Her eyes gleamed with delight. She stroked his shoulders, kissed his chin, and began to undulate beneath him.

"I want more," she murmured before nipping at his neck with sharp teeth.

Curt's fingers tightened on her hips. His laughter was filled with masculine pleasure. He told her she would have to wait, then felt himself hardening as her tongue slipped provocatively in and out of his ear.

"You're a witch," he accused hoarsely as the blood started to pound through his veins again. "A sexy, demanding witch."

Maggie nibbled at his lips. "Do you mind?" she asked.

"No."

_____ TWELVE _____

Later, Maggie drifted to sleep, curled against Curt's chest. His arms enfolded her, and he couldn't seem to take his eyes off her. She was so beautiful, so passionate, so special. The emotions she generated in him were totally foreign.

He'd never wanted a woman the way he wanted Maggie. He'd never strained for the sound of a feminine voice, thrilled at the sound of feminine laughter, or felt warm clear through just at the sight of a woman. He'd never known such gripping jealousy or possessiveness until he'd met her. Was it just the desire?

Would the feelings last? Could they last? Curt doubted it. He didn't know how to sustain a relationship. He'd never wanted to try. His feelings for Maggie were beyond his experience, but that didn't mean they would survive a long-term commitment. He couldn't risk hurting her.

She was too trusting, too open and giving. He wanted to have her near him, but he wouldn't make promises he couldn't keep. He'd spent too many years shunning emotional commitment. He had to be sure that what he was feeling was more than lust, loneliness, or fleeting desire.

What would he do when she decided to leave? She'd promised Rand a year, but the agreement wasn't legally binding. What if she got tired of ranch life once the newness wore off? What if she was offered a more challenging job? How long could he hope to have her near?

Curt brushed damp curls from her face and gently caressed the curve of Maggie's cheek with his thumb. So soft. Her lashes fluttered and slowly lifted. Dreamy brown eyes focused on him with an intimate warmth that knotted Curt's stomach.

Maggie looked into his eyes and her smile deepened. She'd never felt such a wealth of emotion. She loved Curt, but his lovemaking could enslave her for life. He'd been so tender, so passionate, so needy. She ached to tell him how much she loved him, but she didn't want to destroy the peace between them.

"Wow!" Maggie uttered on a husky breath.

Curt's answering smile was wide and pleased. His eyes glittered with possessive warmth. "I think it's safe to say that we're good together."

"Sexually compatible?" she teased.

"Something like that," Curt assured as he brushed a kiss across her nose. "Dynamite."

Maggie giggled, and he pulled her on top of him so that he could hold her closer. She was warm, soft, and womanly. Her thick hair curtained them while they exchanged dozens of tender kisses.

When Maggie began to nibble at Curt's lips with her

teeth, he growled a warning. "Keep that up and you'll be in trouble."

"Hmmm," she murmured. "What kind of trouble?"

"The kind you shouldn't invite if you don't want to be sorry in the morning."

Maggie supposed he was worried about her physical well-being. She'd never felt better in her life. "You're sure I'd be sorry?" she tested, kissing his nose.

Curt laughed. "No. I'm never sure about anything where you're concerned."

Maggie frowned. His tone was teasing, but she knew he was serious about not being sure of her. She hadn't told him how much she cared for him, and she didn't feel comfortable declaring her love until she knew how he felt.

"You can be absolutely sure that I've never shared an experience with anyone that even begins to compare with what we shared tonight."

Curt's eyes grew serious. "I'm glad."

There was a wealth of feeling in those two words. Maggie heard more emotion than Curt had ever expressed outside of his physical desire. The knowledge was encouraging.

"You're very special to me," he added quietly.

Maggie was stunned by the admission. His loving had told her as much, but she was elated that he felt comfortable enough with her to verbalize his feelings. An undying declaration of devotion couldn't have meant more.

"I think you're pretty special, too."

Curt was shaking his head negatively and stroking her hair over her shoulder. "I'm just an average guy, nothing special. My whole world is Oklahoma ranch land. That's the way I always wanted it."

Another warning. Curt was telling her that he'd seen the rest of the world and wasn't interested in it. He probably thought she liked bouncing from city to city, job to job, never really belonging.

"Do you think I'm just going to disappear sometime?" she asked as she rubbed noses with him.

Curt wrapped his arms around her. He didn't even like hearing her say the words. "You promised Rand a year."

"You'll probably be tired of me long before then."

He didn't want to argue the point. He didn't trust his own emotions, but at the minute he didn't think it was possible to get enough of her, let alone too much.

"Curt!" Maggie squealed and thumped his chest with her fist when he didn't immediately refute her words. "You're supposed to lie or sweet-talk me, not just silently concur!"

"I don't want you to get the big head," he teased, rolling them both over and pinning her against the mattress.

"Well, there's certainly no risk of that," she argued petulantly.

Curt kissed her pouting lips until she totally forgot what they'd been talking about. All thoughts were swept from her mind as he continued to steal kiss after kiss, barely giving her a chance to feed air into her lungs. When they were temporarily sated, they dozed off to sleep, wrapped in each other's arms.

Two hours later, Maggie stirred first and glanced at the clock on a stand near the bed. It was 2 A.M. and she knew she had to get moving.

Moaning, she sat up in bed, pulling a sheet around her. A quick glance around the room reminded her that most of her clothing was downstairs.

Maggie's actions bared her back to Curt. He reached out a hand to gently caress the bruised skin, feeling a multitude of conflicting emotions.

"It's not the least bit sore," Maggie insisted before he could make a comment.

"It looks terrible."

"Thanks a bunch," she retorted with flippant sarcasm, trying to tease him and keep the discussion light. "I'm going to get dressed, so you won't have to suffer my terrible looks much longer."

Curt dragged her back against him. "Why are you getting dressed?"

"It's late, or early," Maggie replied, running her hands over his chest. "I have to get home."

"Why?"

She frowned. "I can't stay here all night."

"Why?"

He really didn't understand her reason for leaving. Maggie stuttered an explanation. "It just wouldn't be right . . . or proper . . . or a good idea."

Curt didn't blink an eye. "Why? We've been making love for hours. Are you saying that was wrong and we should hide the fact?"

"No," Maggie argued, pulling out of his arms and wrapping the sheet tighter about her. "But I don't think we need to shout it from the rooftop. It's our business, nobody else's."

"I didn't say I wanted a public announcement," Curt grumbled, hating the way she was already withdrawing from him. "I just want you to stay here. The hell with everybody else."

"My staying here would be tantamount to a public announcement," she said, reaching for her teddy and struggling to don it without releasing the sheet. "You're the one who warned me about ranch gossip. I've managed to keep the men at arm's length. If they find out I spent the night with you, they'll start thinking I'm an easy target. I'd rather be a little more discreet.''

Curt cursed violently under his breath. He didn't want her feeling like she'd cheapened herself by what they'd shared. The thought of other men hitting on her made him see red.

''I'll make sure none of the other men bother you.''

Maggie rose and turned to face him. She'd slipped into her teddy and tossed the sheet back to the bed. ''How can you possibly protect me from gossip and speculation? Mike or Rand would probably defend my honor, too, but nobody's going to say anything in front of them. They won't say anything to you, either, but I'll feel the difference in their attitudes.''

''Then move in with me,'' Curt suggested, climbing from the opposite side of the bed.

Maggie just stared at him. She didn't know what had prompted his suggestion, but she didn't like it. He had tried living with someone before and had ended up hating the other woman. She didn't want to be his next disappointment.

''What purpose would that serve?'' she asked.

''If you're living with me, you won't have to worry about other men bothering you.''

Maggie's temper flared. He didn't say he wanted her to live with him for all the normal reasons, just that he would offer his masculine protection. More macho male reasoning.

''I'll be exclusive property then?'' she challenged.

Curt's features hardened. ''I thought that's what you wanted.'' The idea of any other man touching her made him insane, but he didn't say so.

Maggie sighed and ran her fingers through her tangled hair. "You're right. I'm sorry," she said. "It's frustrating to be a modern woman with old-fashioned ideals. I tell myself that I was brainwashed as a child, but I still can't accept a lot of the liberated standards."

Curt moved around the bed, but didn't touch her. "Does that mean you think tonight was a mistake? One that you don't want to repeat?"

Maggie moved to him and splayed her hands on his chest. Her eyes beseeched him to understand. It was hard to explain without confessing her love.

"I want to be with you as much as possible."

Curt relaxed a little and lifted his hands to her waist. "Then stay with me."

"I know it sounds hypocritical, but I couldn't flaunt convention enough to come and live with you, even if the whole world already knew we're sleeping together."

"Why?"

"It just wouldn't be right," Maggie declared, turning to leave the room. Without a declaration of love from Curt, she wouldn't become a live-in lover.

At the door, she turned to face him again. "I can't explain why, and I don't know if I'll ever change my mind. I won't live with you."

"Will you come back?" The words were hard for Curt.

"As often as possible," Maggie promised.

Curt turned his back on her and reached for a pair of jeans. Maggie went downstairs and gathered her clothing, pulling each article on as she located it.

It was going to be painful to leave. She didn't know if she could bear being parted from Curt for any length of time. Tonight had been incredible. She loved him with an intensity that kept steadily increasing. She was already aching for him and they were still in the same house.

It might be easier to move in with him and forget about the opinion of people like Mike, the McCains, the ranch staff, and her parents. She might not lose their respect, but her own self-respect was at risk.

If Curt had proclaimed his love or a mistrust of marriage, that would be different: she could offer him her love and faith in their relationship until he felt more secure. But without a hint at his true feelings, she just couldn't do it.

What she could do was love him. She knew he didn't have much faith in their relationship. Maybe she'd increased his doubts by refusing to move in with him. It might take her weeks, months, or years, but she would prove that they had a future together. She'd spend so much time here that he'd feel like she did live with him.

Curt entered the living room without a word. He pulled on his shirt and boots, then turned to Maggie. Her beauty caught at his breath and having her leave was tearing him apart.

"I'll drive you home if you're ready."

His tone was totally lacking in emotion. Maggie didn't know if it was a defense mechanism on his part, but it brought tears to her eyes. She lowered her head and concentrated on stepping into her shoes until she was sure her voice would be steady.

"I'm ready," she finally managed. "My coat's on the porch."

Curt's eyes were fastened on her and he saw the sparkle of tears she was trying to hide. The tears tore him apart, but he didn't know what to do or say that would ease her hurt. He'd already offered everything he had to offer and she'd refused him.

They moved to the porch and pulled on coats, being careful not to touch each other. Then they left the house, got in his truck, and traveled the distance to the McCain ranch without a word between them.

Curt pulled to a stop at the ranch entrance closest to Maggie's apartment. He was out of the truck and opening the passenger door before she'd figured out a way to make their parting less painful. She just let instinct rule.

As soon as Curt closed the truck door, she pressed herself close to him and slid her arms around his neck. His reaction was swift and heartening. He wrapped her in his strong arms and drew her closer. His mouth found hers with unerring accuracy. They shared a kiss that was turbulent with emotion. Neither of them wanted it to end. Neither of them really wanted to be parted.

"You could spend the rest of the night with me," Maggie suggested when their lips briefly parted.

The quiet of the night was shattered when two vehicles came racing down the drive and skidded to a stop near the bunk house. The occupants were loud and rowdy, but didn't see Curt's truck at the other side of the main house.

"Mike and the guys must have gotten thrown out of the bar," Maggie whispered lightly.

"Closing time," Curt explained as he brushed a kiss across her forehead. The other men were quickly forgotten.

"So?" Maggie teased. "Would you like to stay with me tonight?" She knew he wouldn't. She didn't even expect him to comment, but she wanted him to understand that it wasn't an easy decision to make.

Curt silently conceded her point. It wouldn't be right for him to stay with her. He couldn't explain, but it just wouldn't be right. She obviously felt the same about moving in with him.

"When can I see you again?" he asked before taking her mouth in another long, lingering kiss.

Maggie was breathless when she finally answered. "How about tomorrow? We don't have to work, so I could come over and have lunch."

"Lunch and supper," Curt insisted, giving her one last kiss before he let her step out of his arms.

"I'll see you about noon," Maggie promised huskily.

"Noon," Curt agreed, then opened the door for her. He made sure she'd locked it before getting back in his truck and driving home.

Maggie spent the next day with Curt and every free minute she could find during the days that followed. They tried not to show any emotion when others were around, but acted like newlyweds when they were alone.

Work was slowing down at the ranch for the winter season, so they had more free time to devote to each other. They spent it laughing, talking, and making love. Maggie fell more deeply in love every time she was with Curt, but neither of them spoke of love or the future.

They were too busy getting to know each other. Maggie shared stories about her childhood, and Curt shared as much as he was able to share about his early life. He told her about dreams of owning his own land and building a home that allowed him plenty of privacy and space. They understood each other's needs to find a home where they felt they really belonged.

With Curt's permission and with much teasing, Maggie began to spread her personal belongings throughout his house. She argued that there was no reason to keep her furniture stored in a corner of the porch when they could be making use of it. Curt argued that she just couldn't be still for two minutes, but he didn't refuse her anything.

Her blue, country print curtains looked perfect in his kitchen. She'd known they would. Her bentwood rocker really was perfect for his living room and so were her colorful throw rugs.

Curt took care of the plumbing and electricity necessary to install her washer and dryer in his laundry room. They moved her bedroom furniture to one of the extra rooms upstairs. Then they made love on her bed, several times, just to make sure they'd reassembled it properly.

November swiftly passed into December. Thanksgiving dinner was shared by the whole ranch family at the main house, then everyone began to think ahead to Christmas. Maggie's parents wanted her to come home for the holiday, and Mike was seriously considering making the trip to Chicago. She didn't even think about leaving Curt at Christmas.

Their time together was precious. Maggie only felt half alive when they were apart. She often saw Curt at the McCain ranch, but he was careful not to say or do anything that might initiate gossip about her.

She didn't know what people were saying or thinking about Curt and her, but she supposed everyone on the ranch was aware of her frequent visits to his house. She didn't care. She was living in a haze of happiness.

The only thing that worried her was Curt's unwillingness to make the first move. There was never any awkwardness between them because she went straight into his arms the minute she entered his house, yet she always made that initial move.

Curt didn't seem to be growing any more secure about her feelings for him. Maggie wished he could learn to trust her, but she knew trust wasn't something that could be rushed. She was determined to earn his trust if it took a lifetime.

By the middle of December, everyone on the ranch was getting caught up in the excitement of the Christmas season. Tara was into her eight month of pregnancy, so Maggie tried to be of more help with the house, with Mindi, and with holiday preparations.

In her free time, she coaxed Curt into letting her decorate his house for the holidays. She knew he didn't have warm memories of the season like she did, but she was determined to create their own special memories. She turned his home into a wonderland of evergreen, holly, and plenty of mistletoe. She won his wholehearted approval of that Christmas tradition.

By the third week of December, all Maggie's extra activities were beginning to take their toll. She was doubling her daytime activities and getting very little sleep. After a very long weekend, she decided not to go to Curt's on Monday evening.

She hoped to catch him sometime during the day, but he was working miles from the house and she didn't see him. He didn't have a phone, so she couldn't call him and let him know not to expect her. She didn't want to send a message over the radio, via Mike or Rand. She was tired, irritable, and decided that she could explain later.

Tuesday wasn't much better. She felt rotten and didn't get a chance to talk with Curt all day. She had a headache, cramps, and wasn't in any mood for company. She didn't go to Curt's house. She felt guilty for not explaining to him, but then reminded herself that he knew exactly where to find her if he was really concerned.

By Wednesday, Maggie was feeling much better. She'd had plenty of rest and her normal energy levels were restored. She was humming cheerfully in the ranch office when the phone interrupted her.

The call was from Jock Carter. He'd been making a pest of himself ever since the night she'd danced with him at the bar. She'd made it clear that she wasn't interested in him, and she'd repeatedly told him not to call her when she was working. He refused to accept the fact that she wasn't thrilled by his attention.

Maggie told him, yet again, that she wouldn't meet him in town and that she didn't want him calling her.

"Now don't be so nasty, honey," Jock said. "It gets awful lonely out here in the winter. Rumor has it that you're already tired of old Hayden, so you shouldn't be so quick to turn down a date with a real man."

Maggie felt the return of a headache aided by a rise in her temper. "You'd be wise to ignore the rumor mill, Mr. Carter, and find yourself another woman to aggravate."

"Easy, honey," Jock drawled.

"Drop dead." Maggie snapped, slamming the receiver down and hoping it hurt his ear. She'd never been so rude in her life, but she'd never met a man more rude and obnoxious.

Her eyes were flashing with fire when she lifted them from the phone and noticed Curt standing very still in the office doorway. The cause of her agitated breathing altered. She wondered how it was possible to miss someone so desperately.

"Hi, cowboy." Her greeting sounded warm and husky. Her smile was intimately warm and welcoming.

THIRTEEN

THIRTEEN

Relief washed over Curt like a tidal wave. The fingers gripping his hat actually trembled. He'd been going out of his mind worrying about her.

"Who was on the other end of that death wish?" he asked, moving into the room and closing the door behind him.

Maggie's brows lifted at his action. He obviously wanted some privacy. She wouldn't complain. "Jock Carter. He's been calling regularly to tell me what a great guy he is and what a fool I am not to be interested."

"You're not interested?" Curt wanted to hear the denial, even though he'd already heard her tell Carter to drop dead.

"I think he's a maggot, but I'd like to know how he found out about you and me."

"You don't really think it's a secret, do you?"

"No, but he said there was a rumor that we weren't seeing each other anymore."

"You haven't been to my house for two nights," Curt reminded, his tone cooling.

Maggie's eyes widened in disbelief. "I imagined the gossips were putting two and two together. I hadn't realized my daily movements were being so closely monitored, or that the information was being shared with everyone within a hundred miles."

"Why haven't you been to my house for the past two nights?" Curt asked. He wasn't interested in the gossip. "Mike just told me you hadn't been feeling well. Why didn't you let me know?"

"I'm fine," Maggie told him. "I was just a little tired. I've been busy with holiday plans. I'm helping Tara redecorate the nursery. It's been hectic around here."

Curt noticed that she didn't look at him while she listed excuses. "How about the truth?"

Maggie felt a blush creeping up her neck. Her eyes were defiant when they met his. "It's just not a good time of the month to come visiting."

She watched the confusion in his eyes turn to comprehension and then annoyance. Curt slowly moved toward her without losing eye contact.

"If you moved in with me, do you think I'd ask you to move out for one week every month?"

Maggie's blush grew warmer. "You might," she hedged. "I'm a real grouch. I feel rotten and that slows me down and that makes me irritable. All I want to do is sleep and eat and snarl at people."

"Or maybe you just don't want to spend time with me unless we can have sex," Curt suggested. His eyes were narrow and watchful.

Maggie's mouth and eyes opened wide with shock. She couldn't believe he would think that. "I was worried about you. I didn't know if you wanted me around if we couldn't . . .'' The word sex didn't make it past her lips.

"Besides," she told him with a saucy grin. "I wasn't quite sure how to broach the subject."

"That has to be a first," said Curt as he stepped very close to her. "I didn't think there was any subject you weren't prepared to argue."

Maggie's breathing grew more shallow as he shortened the distance between them. She could feel the heat of his body. She wanted his arms around her. She wanted his mouth. It would only take a small move by her. He never failed to respond hungrily when she touched him, yet she wanted him to make the first move. It was a small thing, but important.

Curt didn't make her wait long. His hands came up and cupped her face. Then he slowly lowered his head and took her mouth. His tongue delved possessively. The kiss was long, deep, and incredibly sweet.

In his own way, Curt was asking her to have faith in him. Maggie was learning to understand that his actions spoke louder than most men's words. He wasn't just interested in sex, but in everything about her. Joy and relief rushed through her and made her weak.

"I missed you," he murmured when they were forced to draw in air. His arms enfolded her in a tight hug.

Maggie hadn't thought her heart could beat any faster, but it did. She was thrilled by the three little words. He might never say, "I love you," so she valued every small admission of caring.

"I missed you more," she said, her eyes flirting while she argued.

Curt rubbed his lips back and forth over hers. Maggie

thought she heard him mumble "impossible." Then his mouth was coaxing hers open, his tongue delving, the urgency of his kiss wiping all other thoughts from her mind.

A short time later, they heard a tentative knock on the door and gradually allowed their lips to part. Another knock came, followed by Tara's voice.

"Maggie? Is everything all right?"

Curt planted one last kiss on her lips before the door opened and Tara came into the room. She was taken aback when she first saw the couple. The fact that they'd been sharing an embrace didn't surprise her, but the look on Curt's face definitely gave her pause.

Gone was the cool demeanor he usually presented to the world. In its place was soft, adoring eyes and love etched on all his other features. She couldn't wait to tell Rand.

"Should I come back later?"

"No, I've got to get back to work," Curt said as he gave Maggie a smile and picked up his hat. His expression was bland again. "I was just trying to convince Maggie to have supper with me tonight."

Mighty persuasive tactics. Maggie grinned. "Who's cooking and what are we eating?"

"My treat," Curt drawled, his eyes going warm again as he gazed at her smiling features. "TV dinners. The microwaveable kind."

"Yuk!" Maggie wrinkled her nose in disgust. "What time?"

"Anytime you're finished working."

"You're both going to miss Geraldine's pot roast and homemade pecan pie," put in Tara. She needn't have wasted her breath.

"I'll see you about six."

Their eyes met and a current of emotion passed between them. Then Curt nodded a good-bye and left the office.

"Wow," said Tara.

"Yeah, wow," Maggie repeated, still a little dazed by the emotion Curt generated.

"I knew you and Curt were spending a lot of time together, but I didn't realize how serious you were about each other. The temperature in here is definitely fifty degrees warmer than the rest of the house."

Maggie was pretty warm. She gave Tara a smile as the other woman eased her well-rounded body into the chair behind Rand's desk.

"I can't deny that I'm absolutely crazy about the guy," said Maggie. "It's just hard to tell how serious he is about me."

"You mean he hasn't told you?"

"He's a man of few words."

"I know," chided Tara, "but the way he looks at you is a testimony in itself. There's no doubt in my mind that the man's madly in love with you. I wouldn't have imagined it possible, but you can almost see Cupid's arrow piercing his heart."

Maggie laughed softly, yet her eyes were serious. She'd never discussed her feelings for Curt with anyone, but she needed reassurance. "You've known him longer than I have. Do you really think there's a chance he could love me and accept me in his life for an extended period of time?"

Tara started to make a teasing remark, but realized that Maggie was anxious and uncertain. "I really don't know Curt all that well. I know he's a very private person. I used to think he hated women, but he probably just never met a woman who cared enough to teach him about love."

"I care enough," said Maggie.

Tara gave her a smile. "Then your future's looking bright, because I'd be willing to bet all the pecans in the world that he cares as much for you."

Maggie relaxed a little and laughed. Tara's constant craving for pecans was driving Rand crazy, and had become a household joke. The other woman's evaluation of Curt's feelings were encouraging.

The phone rang and Tara automatically answered it, frowned, and silently mouthed the name Jock Carter to Maggie. Maggie vigorously shook her head.

"I'm sorry, Jock, she can't come to the phone. Can I take a message?"

Tara rolled her eyes, but remained polite. When she broke the connection, she passed the message on to Maggie.

"Jock says that his invitation still stands. His tone implied that you'd be wise not to turn down the opportunity to spend time with him."

"Yuk!"

Tara grinned at her comic expression. "I know how you feel. He's attractive, but so conceited that he's unbearable when he's sober. When he's drinking, he can be really mean and ugly. If you'd like, I'll have Rand say something to Craig. I know he's given Jock several warnings."

"I don't want to cause him to lose his job or anything like that," said Maggie. She imagined he'd carry quite a grudge. "I just wish he'd direct his attention elsewhere."

"That's not likely as long as you're interested in Curt," Tara explained. "Rand told me that Jock was having an affair with a woman from Larson a few years ago. Then the woman met Curt and didn't want anything to do with Jock. Rand didn't think Curt paid any attention to Jock's girlfriend, but she eventually moved out of state."

"And Jock blamed Curt?"

"I suppose," replied Tara. "The poor woman probably grasped at any excuse to escape Jock."

"I can understand that," said Maggie.

The phone rang again. This time it was for Tara and Maggie went back to work at her computer. She wiped the thought of Jock Carter from her mind and concentrated on livestock files. The sooner she got finished, the sooner she could see Curt.

By Saturday evening, Maggie was feeling happier than she'd ever felt in her life. Curt loved her. She knew he loved her as much as she loved him. His tenderness and attentiveness had proven how much he cared, even if he didn't make promises.

Christmas was just a few days away and that added to Maggie's festive mood. She and Tara had spent the day shopping in Oklahoma City. She'd bought Curt a gold watch, but had immediately thrown the price tag in the trash. She didn't want him to have a clue to how much she'd spent, she just wanted something special for him.

She'd bought him an electric train set and a radio-controlled car. The man was learning how to play, so she wanted to continue his education. She wanted plenty of brightly colored packages under his tree on Christmas morning.

Her attire for the evening was new, too, from the lacy underclothes to the soft cashmere of the form-fitting dress. The yellow suited her coloring, making her complexion look creamy and her eyes look mysteriously dark.

Maggie grinned at her reflection in the mirror and dabbed perfume behind her ears and at her wrists. Then she grabbed her purse and coat before heading to the front of the house to tell Tara she was leaving.

The other woman was looking very pregnant and miserable. She was sitting on the sofa with her legs propped up, but she didn't look the least bit comfortable.

"Are you okay?" asked Maggie.

"I feel rotten."

"We did too much today, didn't we?"

"Probably," Tara agreed with a snort. "It's not your fault, though. I'm the one who insisted we keep shopping after you suggested we stop."

"Can I do anything to make you more comfortable?"

Rand had taken Mindi and Geraldine to visit at a ranch north of his while he conducted some business. Tara would be alone if she left. "Maybe I'd better stay until Rand gets back."

"Please don't!" Tara coaxed. "I promise I'm not going to move a muscle, and there's nothing that will make me more comfortable until I rest a while. Rand won't be long, then I can play on his sympathy and talk him into giving me a back rub."

The mischievous smile on Tara's face made Maggie grin. Then the phone rang and they both grimaced.

"One of these days, I'm going to tear that thing right out of the wall!" said Tara.

Maggie stepped into the hallway and answered the annoying summons, then strained to hear the voice at the other end. There was a lot of background noise and static in the line.

"This is Curt," said a rough voice.

"Curt," Maggie's voice warmed. "I can hardly hear you." She'd never talked to him on the phone before, but he sounded strange and distant.

"A change of plans for tonight," he said in a voice so low that Maggie had to cover her left ear in hopes of hearing better from her right ear.

"What kind of change?" she asked.

"I want you to meet me in town."

Maggie wasn't sure she heard him right, the background noise had gotten louder. "Where are you? Did you say you want me to come to town?"

"Come to the bar. I have a surprise for you."

"The same bar where Mike took me?"

"Yeah, hurry."

There was more static and the line went dead. Maggie frowned at the telephone receiver.

"What's wrong?" asked Tara when she saw the frown.

"That was Curt, but it was a really bad connection. He said he's at the bar and he wants me to meet him there."

"That doesn't sound like Curt."

"He said he had a surprise for me," replied Maggie. "Maybe he wants to show off his new dance techniques," she added with a grin. She and Curt had been doing a lot of practicing. Maybe he thought she'd enjoy an evening on the town, such as it was.

"Curt dances at the bar?" Tara asked in surprise.

Maggie laughed at Tara's wide-eyed disbelief. "We haven't advanced to the bar and lounge dancing stage, but he's very skillful," she teased, her eyes sparkling.

Tara just grunted and propped another pillow behind

her back. "I'm afraid that dancing of any sort doesn't hold much appeal for me right now."

"Are you sure there's nothing I can do for you?"

"I'm positive. I'm just going to take a nap before Rand gets home. I'll need the strength to endure his lectures about pushing myself too hard."

Maggie pulled an afghan from the back of a nearby chair and covered Tara, tucking the edges around her wide girth. Then she picked up her coat and slipped her arms through the sleeves.

"If Rand doesn't get home soon and you start feeling worse, just call me," Maggie told her as she headed for the door.

"Will do," promised Tara before she closed her eyes with a sigh. Sleep came swiftly.

The next time Tara opened her eyes, Rand was entering the house. He was followed by Geraldine, Mindi, Mike, and Curt. She expected Maggie to be next, but Curt closed the door behind him.

"Where's Maggie?" she asked, still groggy from her nap.

"I hope she's here," said Curt. "We have a date tonight."

His statement made Mindi giggle, but Tara put her feet on the floor and sat up straighter.

"She was headed to your house, but then she got a phone call from you."

"Not from me," said Curt, his eyes narrowing in concern.

Tara was beginning to get concerned, too. "Someone told her it was you. She said the connection was really bad, but that you wanted her to meet you at the bar."

"The bar?" Curt, Rand, Mike, and Geraldine chorused the question in a variety of tones.

"I'll go check on her," Mike declared.

Curt was already headed for the door. "I'll find her."

Mike started to follow, but Mindi was hanging on his legs, oblivious of the sudden tension in the room. He lifted her and handed her to her dad.

"Curt'll let us know if he needs us," said Rand as he took Mindi to the stairway and told her to head upstairs to get ready for bed.

Mike frowned and Tara couldn't resist teasing him. "I've heard it's really hard when your babies finally spread their wings and leave the nest."

She was right. For most of Maggie's life, he'd been her protector. It was hard to accept the fact that she might not need him anymore. She had Curt now.

"Just wait, little mother," he threatened. "I'm gonna be right here when your babies take flight, and I'm gonna remind you of your heartless teasing."

The phone was ringing again and Tara held a pillow over her head. Rand answered, asked the caller a few terse questions, and then ended the conversation. His expression was grim.

"That was Craig. Jock Carter went on a drinking binge, started fighting everybody in sight, and got himself fired. After he left, one of Craig's other men told him that Jock was swearing vengeance on Curt. Craig was worried."

"So am I," said Tara. "That could have been Jock on the phone telling Maggie to come to town. She had no reason to think it was anybody but Curt."

"We'd better follow Curt. If he hurts Maggie, Curt'll kill him," said Rand.

"If Curt doesn't, I will," Mike snarled, already

heading for the door. Rand gave Tara a quick kiss and followed him.

Curt was halfway to town, with the gas pedal to the floor on a long stretch of straight road. Someone had lured Maggie to town. It made him livid without knowing who or why. He didn't want anybody messing with his Maggie.

Two distant headlights appeared a few miles down the road, heading toward Curt. The lights were small, close together, and low to the ground. It looked like Maggie's car, and he eased the pressure on his accelerator a little.

Then another set of headlights suddenly appeared out of the darkness at the edge of the road, closer to the oncoming car than to Curt's truck. He swore viciously, feeling an instant of impotent rage before the third vehicle lurched onto the road, directly in the path of the oncoming sports car.

Curt hit his brakes and watched in slow-motion horror as the small car swerved wildly to avoid a head-on collision. There was no way around the other vehicle, except to run off the road.

The offending vehicle was a truck, and its bigger headlights shone on the small car just long enough for Curt to be sure it was Maggie. She hit the graveled berm, and then her car dipped as she hit a shallow ditch.

The next thing he knew, her car was rolling, cartwheeling end over end at a high rate of speed. Gravel, dirt, sparks, and glass flew in every direction as the sports car tumbled forward across an open field, its headlights and taillights doing a sickening somersault until they were finally crushed and extinguished. Every muscle in his body tightened painfully.

"No!" Curt roared as he drove off the same side of
the road and stopped just yards from where her car had
come to an abrupt halt. He was out of the truck and
running toward her before the dust had cleared, but still
it wasn't fast enough.

"No! No! No!" he yelled in an anguished cry. The
fear was sharp and gripping. His heart and lungs knotted in terror. Not Maggie. Not sweet Maggie. Please
not Maggie.

His body was rigid from shock, so rigid that his
limbs felt weighted and uncoordinated. He couldn't run
fast enough. He had to mentally command his body to
function. The commands were all that saved him from
total panic. Hurry. Hurry. Go faster. Get to her. Help
her. Help her. Get her out of that car.

"Maggie!" he yelled as he reached the driver's side
of the car and felt the heat rolling off the hot metal. In
a tortured tone, he repeated his call, "Maggie!"

His truck lights offered some illumination. All the
windows of the car were shattered. The top was crushed
nearly to the steering wheel and Maggie was crushed
under it. Curt hadn't prayed for thirty years, but he
alternately prayed and cursed.

He couldn't open her door. It was locked from the
inside; but without a window, he was able to release
the lock and forcefully pry the door open. He fell on
his knees to reach beyond Maggie and shut off the
engine. He smelled gasoline fumes and felt the suffocat-
ing heat rising from the car's engine.

As he leaned into the car, he saw blood on her face
and felt fear curl tighter in his stomach. He couldn't
tell if she was breathing.

"Maggie!" If she could have heard him, she'd have
had no doubt about the depths of his feelings for her.

His tone was agonized as he tried to rouse her to consciousness while he struggled to reach the latch on her seat belt.

If he moved her and she had a serious head or back injury, he could paralyze or kill her. If he didn't move her and the car exploded, she'd be burned alive. Primitive instinct urged him to get her as far away from the car as possible.

Thick smoke began to roll from under the car's hood. Curt slipped both arms under Maggie and tried to slowly and gently slide her from the mangled wreckage of her car.

When she was safely in his arms, he straightened and got a more secure grip on her limp body. He carried her through a haze of smoke toward the lights of his truck. The crackle of fire taunted him from behind, and he covered the ground to safety more swiftly.

He was assaulted by the acrid smell of gasoline as he laid Maggie on the ground, covering her body with his own when the sports car's engine erupted in flames and then exploded, sending glass and hot shards of metal flying through the air with deadly force.

Curt's denim jacket and heavy clothing protected him from any flying particles and he protected Maggie. When the force of the initial explosion was passed, he rolled to her side and began to check her for serious injuries. Unbuttoning her coat, he reached inside and felt the gentle rise and fall of her chest.

She was alive. Relief rushed over him and his hands trembled. "Maggie. Maggie, sweetheart, talk to me," he coaxed in a deeply husky voice. "Please, baby, wake up and talk to me."

He brushed her hair from her face. He could see the cut on her head that blood was trickling from. It didn't look too wide or deep, but he didn't know how hard a blow she'd suffered.

She was covered with crushed glass; it was in her hair, in her eyes, nose, and on her lips. When he carefully brushed the particles from her eyes, her lashes fluttered, and then her eyelids rose. Her eyes were dark and confused.

"Curt?"

A shudder ripped through him at the sound of his name. His throat was tight and clogged. When he finally spoke, his voice was low and rough.

"I'm right here, honey. You had an accident, but you're safe now. Where do you hurt?"

She lifted her head slightly, saw the burning inferno that used to be her car, remembered the sickening roll, and dropped her head back to the ground.

"Maggie?" Curt repeated hoarsely. Fear still had a stranglehold on him. She could have a serious head injury and internal damage. He carefully brushed more glass from her, wanting to crush her in his arms, but afraid to.

"Where do you hurt?"

It was a long, painful moment before she answered. "Everywhere, I think." Her voice was steady, her mind clear.

Another shudder rocked Curt. His eyes stung. If he hadn't been insane with worry, he would have been amused. "Does any place hurt more than the others?"

Maggie shifted and groaned. The next thing he heard was the sound of a truck approaching at a high rate of speed. Curt immediately spread his body over hers, looked toward the road, and realized it was Rand.

Mike was out of the truck before Rand had come to a complete stop. "Maggie!" he yelled as he saw her

car in the flames. "Maggie!" It was the roar of a
wounded bear.

Curt tried to call out to him, but his throat was still
tight and he didn't trust it. When Rand turned his headlights on the accident scene, Curt waved an arm to alert
him to their whereabouts.

"Curt's got her, Mike! I'll call Craig and get the
helicopter out here!" Rand yelled to the big man who
was already halfway to the flaming wreckage. Mike
turned abruptly, located the couple and came racing to
Maggie's side. He dropped to the ground and carefully
captured one of her hands in his.

"Midget?"

"I'm okay, Michael," she responded quietly, squeezing his fingers. Strength was flooding back into her
bruised limbs, but she had a feeling that her two tough
guys were about to fall to pieces on her.

Mike lifted his worried eyes from her just an instant
to give Curt a brief perusal. "Are you all right?"

"I wasn't in danger," Curt told him gruffly, but
knew it was a lie. If Maggie hurt, he hurt. If she'd
died, part of him, maybe the best part, would have died
with her.

Life without her held no appeal, Curt realized.

"Craig's got a back board on the copter. He can
fly her to Oklahoma City faster than we can get an
ambulance."

"I don't want to go to the hospital," Maggie protested. With her returning strength came a return of
spirit. She tested her limbs for feeling and mobility. "I
just have a bump on my head and a few bruises. I'm
sure nothing is seriously hurt."

"We'll let the doctors decide that," Curt injected,
his tone strong and firm again.

"Mike's a doctor," she blurted without thinking. "He can check for broken bones and concussion."

Curt's eyes went to Mike's. The big man was already running his hands over her to check for any obvious injury.

"I'm a psychiatrist, not a trauma doctor. You need X-rays and a thorough examination."

"Damn!" Maggie retorted. "You won't leave me, will you?" she asked Curt, clutching his hand.

"I'll be as close as I can get," he replied, brushing a kiss across her lips. Maggie returned the kiss, and then had to spit a stray shard of glass out of her mouth. She wanted to sit up. She wanted Curt's arms around her.

"Lay still," Mike commanded.

"Lie still," she corrected irritably.

"Who was that maniac who ran me off the road?"

Curt wasn't sure. Mike was fairly sure. Neither of them commented, and Maggie knew whoever the idiot was, he'd wish he'd never been born if her guys found him before the sheriff. She didn't feel a bit of sympathy for him. He'd ruined her special evening, he'd destroyed her car, and worse.

"I just bought this outfit," she wailed. "And my car is destroyed!"

"Now don't go getting hysterical on us," Mike told her gruffly, concerned that she might go into shock.

Curt shifted long enough to let Mike complete his check of her limbs, then his arm was around Maggie again. The helicopter was nearing and Mike went to help Rand clear an area for landing.

Maggie reached a hand to Curt's face and caressed his cheek. "Did you save my life?"

"Probably." His eyes were dark with concern, but

he managed a light, teasing tone. "I guess that makes us even."

"Nope," she argued, drawing his head closer to feel the comfort of his lips on hers. "That means we belong to each other, forever."

FOURTEEN

"Well, young woman, your tests are all clear, no serious damage," said Dr. Henley, a physician at the hospital where Mike and Curt had brought her.

"I tried to tell these guys I was fine, but they wouldn't pay any attention," said Maggie, with a glance at her two big protectors.

She'd been examined and X-rayed in the emergency room, then put to bed in a private room. She'd gotten a good night's sleep. Mike and Curt hadn't been so lucky. They looked like hell this morning and she'd already told them so.

"I'm glad they brought you in. It's a good idea to keep all accident victims under observation for a few hours."

"When can I go home?"

Dr. Henley was another big Oklahoma man with sharp eyes and a sense of humor. He tried to scowl but ended up grinning.

"You sound a bit impatient to leave."

"No offense, doctor, but I didn't want to come in the first place. I was bullied," Maggie declared. She looked like a fragile doll in her shapeless hospital gown, but her eyes gleamed with mischief. "It's the story of my life."

"And a woeful tale it is," he agreed, giving her a wink that said he knew she was much loved. "I think someone brought you clean clothes. I'll sign your release and you can split this joint."

Maggie laughed, her eyes sparkling as she reached out a hand to the doctor. He shook it firmly and bid them a good day.

Mike stepped to the bed. He'd been hovering close since Maggie's breakfast was delivered an hour earlier. Curt was on the opposite side of her bed, a few steps from her side, near the room's only window. He'd been quiet except to ask if she was feeling all right this morning. Still, Maggie was intensely aware of his presence and his concern.

"Craig flew me back to the ranch last night and I got you some clothes. Then I drove one of Rand's cars here to take you home. It shouldn't be too uncomfortable."

"I'll be fine, big guy," she repeated for the tenth time. "My seat belt protected me from serious injury. I'm feeling stiff and little sore, but I'm fine. I don't even have a headache."

"Rand talked to the sheriff. If you weren't so short, your skull would have been crushed."

"I'm pleased to know that, Dr. Craton. Your bedside manner definitely needs some work."

Mike frowned. His first visit to a hospital since he'd left his profession was proving difficult.

"Why don't you go have a long chat with the medical staff while I get dressed," Maggie suggested.

"Do you want me to send in a nurse to help?" he asked.

"I'd rather you tell them to give me some privacy," she said, her eyes meeting Curt's. She needed to talk to him. He'd been so quiet. His eyes rarely left her, but she feared he was constructing barriers again.

Mike gave her a brief kiss on the cheek. "I'll take care of all the paperwork and be back in about an hour."

"Thanks."

The room seemed unbearably quiet when he left. It was a bright, cheerful room, but the tension between the remaining occupants was heavy. Curt moved closer to the side of the bed and Maggie held her breath.

His jeans and shirt showed the ravages of his rescue efforts. He had a night's growth of beard and his eyes looked haunted. The tight expression on his face troubled Maggie.

"Did you get any sleep last night?" she asked, reaching a hand to him.

Curt grasped it and brought it to his lips, kissing her palm and then each of her fingers. "I didn't want to sleep," he said. He hadn't wanted to take his eyes off her.

Maggie's pulse accelerated. She loved him so much. His lightest touch and the sound of his voice were enough to make her giddy with pleasure.

"Did I thank you for saving my life?"

Curt didn't respond. He eased his body onto her bed, his eyes capturing hers. "I almost went out of my mind when I saw your car roll across that field."

There was so much pain in his eyes that it brought

tears to hers. She reached out her arms and was lifted into his lap.

"You're really all right?" Curt asked as he nuzzled her neck. "It won't hurt if I hold you?" He badly needed to.

"Only if you don't hold me tight enough," Maggie insisted, hugging him fiercely and pressing her mouth to the strong, pulsing vein of his neck.

Curt's arms tightened. He held her close and buried his face in her hair. She was alive and well. He needed a kiss. His lips searched until he found her mouth. Then he showed her how relieved he was with kiss after hungry kiss.

Maggie didn't know how anybody could be so gentle, yet so obviously needy. The emotion pouring from Curt's body to hers made her feel weak and weepy. He wasn't going to draw into his protective shell. He was offering his heart, whether he realized it or not.

"Don't you dare scare me like that again," Curt commanded gruffly.

Maggie drew back and grinned at him. "I thought I was being obedient by racing to meet you in town. Then when I got to the bar, you weren't there, and the bartender said you never had been."

Curt's expression was murderous for an instant. "Carter set up the whole thing. He lured you to town and then waited for you to head home alone."

Maggie smoothed the frown lines from his forehead. "I'm sure Rand and the sheriff will take care of him," she said, then her brow creased in a frown. "I suppose he's an uninsured motorist."

Curt grinned. His eyes sparkled with love. He adored her. "I want to marry you," he told her calmly, though his stomach knotted with apprehension and his fingers tightened on the soft skin of her waist.

Maggie's heart leapt to her throat. She was taken completely by surprise. Her eyes searched his. She wanted the same thing, but not because of an impulsive decision that he might later regret.

"Why?" she forced herself to ask him.

"I love you," he told her with quiet sincerity.

"I know," she breathed softly, her eyes shining with adoration. "I love you, too. But that doesn't explain your change of heart about long-term commitment."

Curt savored her declaration of love for a moment as he brushed his lips over hers. He knew she loved him. She'd taught him all about love in the past few weeks, but she'd never given him the words. Now that she had, she wanted to be difficult about marriage.

"Last night, when you were hurt and I wanted to be near you, the hospital staff kept trying to shove me aside because I didn't have any legal right to stay with you."

Judging by the tone of his voice, the hospital staff had learned that he wasn't an easy man to handle.

"First you want exclusive rights, now you want legal rights?" she challenged boldly. "Are you sure those are good enough reasons to get married?"

Curt's eyes narrowed and his expression was tight. Sometimes his lady love drove him crazy with her argumentative attitude. "We love each other. Isn't that enough reason?" he growled.

It was enough. Maggie was willing to take whatever she could get from him, but she wanted to understand why he'd finally proposed. She didn't want him to harbor any doubts.

"What about your independent life? What about all those dreams of space and privacy?"

Curt laid her on the bed and pressed her gently against the mattress with his big body. He rested his weight on his elbows. One hand clutched her hair. He used the other hand to stroke her cheek.

Maggie knew he was searching for words to express how he felt. It might be hard for him, but the anticipation nearly killed her. Her heart was racing. She silently pleaded with him to make her believe.

"I've been having some new dreams lately," Curt finally managed, steadily returning her dark gaze.

"Really?" Maggie barely dared to breathe.

Curt nodded and kissed her. Then he drew back and explained. "I keep seeing images of red-haired baby girls with big brown eyes and sassy smiles."

"Babies!" Maggie grew breathless with excitement. Her eyes widened, searching his intently. She knew he wouldn't even mention babies unless he was totally committed to a relationship and trusted her implicitly.

"Do you mean it? Would you really like to get married and have a family?" she whispered.

"I might like you all to myself for a while," he teased, elated by her reaction.

"Oh, Curt!" she cried, throwing her arms around him and taking the full weight of his body until he enveloped her with his strong arms. "I love you so much!"

"I love you more," he argued as he took her lips for a long, sweet kiss. "Are you going to marry me?"

Maggie was light-headed with relief and a mixture of thrilling emotions: love, happiness, wild excitement.

"I'll give it some serious consideration," she teased

playfully, running her hands up his neck to grip his head.

"You really are a sassy brat, you know."

His words were accompanied by a string of hot, open-mouthed kisses that made all her nerve endings tingle.

"Who says?"

SHARE THE FUN . . .
SHARE YOUR NEW-FOUND TREASURE!!

You don't want to let your new books out of your sight? That's okay. Your friends can get their own. Order below.

No. 50 RENEGADE TEXAN by Becky Barker
Rane lives only for himself—that is, until he meets Tamara.

No. 57 BACK IN HIS ARMS by Becky Barker
Fate takes over when Tara shows up on Rand's doorstep again.

No. 58 SWEET SEDUCTION by Allie Jordan
Libby wages war on Will—she'll win his love yet!

No. 59 13 DAYS OF LUCK by Lacey Dancer
Author Pippa Weldon finds her real-life hero in Joshua Luck.

No. 60 SARA'S ANGEL by Sharon Sala
Sara *must* get to Hawk. He's the only one who can help.

No. 61 HOME FIELD ADVANTAGE by Janice Bartlett
Marian shows John there is more to life than just professional sports.

No. 62 FOR SERVICES RENDERED by Ann Patrick
Nick's life is in perfect order until he meets Claire!

No. 63 WHERE THERE'S A WILL by Leanne Banks
Chelsea goes toe-to-toe with her new, unhappy business partner.
